INSIDE THE INDIE HORROR WORLD

PRESENTED BY KEVIN J. KENNEDY

FEATURING THOUGHTS, STORIES AND ADVICE FROM

DAVID MOODY S.E. ENGLAND SIMON CLARK
MERCEDES M. YARDLEY MARK LUKENS
JOHN EVERSON CHAD LUTSKE
AND MANY MORE

Inside the Indie Horror World

KJK Publishing

Inside the Indie Horror World © 2023 Kevin J. Kennedy

Edited by Ann Keeran & Kevin J. Kennedy

Cover design by Michael Bray

All rights reserved. No part of this publication may be reproduced, distributed, or transmitted in any form or by any means, including photocopying, recording, or other electronic or mechanical methods, without the prior written permission of the publisher, except in the case of brief quotations embodied in critical reviews and certain other non-commercial uses permitted by copyright law.

First Printing, 2023

Other Books by KJK Publishing

Collections
Dark Thoughts
Vampiro and Other Strange Tales of the Macabre
Merry Fuckin' Christmas and Other Yuletide Shit!
The A to Z of Horror

Anthologies
Collected Christmas Horror Shorts
Collected Easter Horror Shorts
Collected Halloween Horror Shorts
Collected Christmas Horror Shorts 2
The Horror Collection: Gold Edition
The Horror Collection: Black Edition
The Horror Collection: Purple Edition
The Horror Collection: White Edition
The Horror Collection: Silver Edition
The Horror Collection: Pink Edition
The Horror Collection: Emerald Edition
The Horror Collection: Pumpkin Edition
The Horror Collection: Yellow Edition
The Horror Collection: Ruby Edition
The Horror Collection: Extreme Edition
The Horror Collection: Nightmare Edition
The Horror Collection: Sapphire Edition
The Horror Collection: The Lost Edition

The Horror Collection: LGBTQIA+ Edition
100 Word Horrors
100 Word Horrors 2
100 Word Horrors 3
100 Word Horrors 4
Carnival of Horror

Novels and Novellas
Pandemonium by J.C. Michael
You Only Get One Shot by Kevin J. Kennedy & J.C. Michael
Screechers by Kevin J. Kennedy & Christina Bergling
Stitches by Steven Stacy & Kevin J. Kennedy
Halloween Land by Kevin J. Kennedy

Dedication

I'd like to dedicate this book to every single indie horror fan out there. We love you!

Table of Contents

History of the Horror Novel
Lee McGeorge

A Dangerous Passage
Russell R. James

12 Point, Times New Roman
David Moody

Back When I Was a Kid….
John Everson

Living the Pipe Dream
Brian Moreland

Developing Your Writing Process
Tom Deady

Chase Those Nightmares
John Durgin

Welcome to the Community
Natasha Sinclair

Don't do me any Favors
Mark Allan Gunnells

Some Tips for the new (Indie Horror) Author
Kenzie Jennings

Choosing a Publisher
Chad Lutzke

Diary of A Dreamer
Jim Ody

Change the Music, Keep the Melody
Brennan LaFaro

Paint it Dark
~ Creating an eerie atmosphere and foreshadowing ominous events ~
Simon Clark

Free Therapy
Mark Towse

Hey, Hi. You're Never Going to be Good Enough.
Mercedes M. Yardley

Writer's Firsts of a Long Journey
Eric J. Guignard

Time Is A River That Is Sometimes Still
John Boden

Learning to Write Happy
Alex Laybourne

Memoirs of an Indie Idiot
Adam Millard

Writing Questions. Writing Answers
Gage Greenwood

Double-edged
Christina Bergling

We Are Not Alone
Jay Bower

Bleed Through the Microphone
Patrick R. McDonough

Shaping a Legacy
Joe Mynhardt

Write from the Heart
Sarah E. England

Writing to Market
Ash Ericmore

Rest if You Must, But Don't You Quit
R.E. Sargent

These Hybrid Moments
Robert Essig

Advice From Steve
Steve Stred

So, I wrote a book, now what?
Candace Nola

10 Steps to Becoming an Author
Mark Lukens

The Killer Mentality
Nick Roberts

Success?

John R. Little

Foreword

Most of the people in this book are authors but most of them have other focuses in the horror world too. There are CEO's of multiple publishers in the book. Think about that for a minute. KJK Publishing is releasing this book and yet the guys that run their own horror publishing companies were still willing to take part and share advice and stories with you. Others talk about this in more depth in the book, but I think it displays what the horror community has to offer. Should we be competing? Should we be enemies, trying to get horror fans from the other company, or should we all just get along and share in our love of horror. It's much more fun when everyone plays nice.

I've been part of the horror world for over seven years now. I have released around thirty anthologies, 4 solo short story collections, a solo novella and several co-written novellas. I've had stories in God knows how many anthologies by other publishers, had stories translated into Italian and Japanese. I've appeared in books alongside most of my favourite writers, had a ridiculous amount of Amazon chart toppers and I get to read a tonne of short horror stories by my favourite horror authors before anyone else. When I write it down, it seems a little mental.

I run a publishing company and I write from time to time but in reality, I put horror books together for myself and hope that others have similar taste to me. I read Point Horror books when I was a kid and when I was fifteen, I found my first adult horror book in Richard Laymon's Darkness Tell Us. It blew me away. I could not put it down. From memory, it was about 600 pages, but I flew through it in 3 days. Next up I read Island, also by Laymon and then I worked through his entire catalogue. I ended up on the Laymon message board and I was introduced to several other authors. A lot of these authors at the time were releasing books mostly through small presses or Leisure Publishing. I had to buy everything on Amazon because you just couldn't find these books in the UK but I became a fan of indie fiction or small press fiction in the early days of Amazon when it was basically an online book store. I never returned to mass market books. Now, years later, I take for granted what the industry has done for me. I am a part of it. Every single day I am either reading submissions for a book, editing, formatting, advertising, promoting, pitching a new idea to authors, and the list goes on. I put a lot of time into it, but it never feels like an effort. Well... maybe the editing.

Until this point everything I have released has been fictional. I speak to a lot of authors and thought it would be interesting to get them all together and tell some stories, give some advice and tell you a little bit about the world that we are all trying to navigate in one way or another. This book is not a 'How to,' book. It is a book with hints, tips and advice but more than that, it's a look at the lives of the individuals who entertain us all. Those that we look to in our relaxation time to take our minds away to another place. This book is the most intimate book I have put together to date. I am humbled that the community opened up and shared their stories with me, and now I get to share them with the rest of you.

Thank you to everyone who made this project possible and thank you to those who have picked up a copy. We hope you enjoy the tour.

Kevin J. Kennedy

History of the Horror Novel
By
Lee McGeorge

Did you ever wonder where horror began? I mean, as an entertainment medium, as a product designed to scare us? Where did the first horror novels come from?

The earliest books that would equate to horror writing were guides to defeating witches that appeared around the seventeenth century. These guidebooks were essentially short stories written up as titillating self-help guides, but they weren't what a modern reader would call a novel. So where do they begin? Scholars and historians can point to a multitude of books from the gothic era that gave birth to the genre, but here are five books that I think were the game changers that shaped the genre.

First on that list is The Castle of Otranto (1764) by Horace Walpole. 'Castle' opens with the handsome young Conrad about to marry his love, Isabella, until a giant metal helmet falls from the sky and crushes his head. Conrad's father and lord of the castle, Manfred, is terrified by the death of his son as it had been prophesied he would die without an heir. In his panic to avoid the prophecy coming true,

Manfred chases the hapless Isabella around the castle intent on raping her so that she may fall pregnant, thus foiling the prophecy.

It's bonkers; and sadly, like many age-old texts, is borderline unreadable to modern audiences; but this eighteenth century potboiler was the unstoppable bestseller in its day. Whilst The Castle of Otranto is far from being a horror novel, it stands out vividly for being fantastical. Writers of that age were striving for realism. Flights of fantasy and imagination were considered unworthy of a serious writer but Walpole disagreed, musing that if Shakespeare could comfortably write about ghosts and witches, why couldn't he?

Because 'Castle' was such a runaway hit, it set the mood and appetite for more fantastical literature. Other writers jumped on the bandwagon and began adding ghosts and phantasms and the supernatural to their gothic and romantic stories; but 'Castle' was definitely the first.

The next book to push the creation of horror forward did so by adding gore and shock to the storytelling. The French Revolution had begun in 1789 and as news of the peasants' revolt began to spread it was seen as the rich getting their just deserts; but then rumors started of terrifying barbarity. There were shocking reports that the peasants had invented a mechanism that severed limbs and heads. It was an unspeakable evil. The peasants had invented a killing machine and, as word of its use spread, the blood and guts began filtering into literature.

The book to capitalize on this carnage was The Monk (1796) written by nineteen year old Matthew Gregory Lewis. A story of illicit sex, cross-dressing, rape, pregnant nuns, murder, ghostly apparitions, dead and decaying babies, burning people at the stake, matricide, incest and even summoning up the devil. (Before you get your hopes up, this too is borderline unreadable to modern audiences.) The Monk closed out the eighteenth century by showing the extreme and was a giant leap forward for horror literature.

The genre now had fantasy, violence and was unafraid to shock, but its next major step was going to add one of the most evocative of horror leanings. Prescience. Horror was about to capture the anxiety of the day and in the early nineteenth century fear came from science. As experimenters began to solve the mysteries of the world, society began to consider that science would eventually conquer death and return the dead to the world of the living. In literature, nothing captured this anxiety quite like Mary Shelley's, Frankenstein or The Modern Prometheus (1818).

At the time of publication, medicine and medical technology was at the forefront of the sciences but there weren't enough cadavers for student doctors to practice on. Medical schools were desperate for corpses and offered such huge sums that grave-robbing became a lucrative trade. Barely a cemetery in Europe or America was untouched and it's easy to see why the public latched on to Shelley's dark fantasy. Whilst modern audiences think of Victor Frankenstein's monster as being the horror, the terror that beguiled the reading masses of the day was the out-of-control scientist who would steal you from your grave and mutilate you after death, or even worse, reanimate your decayed corpse. Frankenstein got under people's skin. There really were grave robbers and mad scientists out there and they terrified people. That terror was captured in literature and makes Frankenstein my third game changer.

For game changers four and five I'm going to look at vampires. There is a wealth of literature on vampires that begin with a collection of non-fiction essays under the title "Dissertations Upon the Apparitions of Angels, Daemons, and Ghosts, and Concerning the Vampires of Hungary, Bohemia, Moravia, and Silesia" (1746). The vampire as an entertainment product began to take shape in 1819 through John William Polidori's short tale, The Vampyre but it still wasn't really a horror novel. Over the next fifty years, vampires and vampire stories began to form and borrow from one another, but our first real novel to be rocking a sensual, blood sucker is Carmilla (1872), created by Joseph Sheriden Le Fanu.

Carmilla is a lesbian vampire who sexually desires a young girl; she seduces the girl's mother to get close to the daughter, then when the mother has fallen in love and lowers her guard, Carmilla steals the daughter and abandons the love-struck mother. What a scandalous shocker this must have been in the Victorian age. With its mix of horror, sex and lesbian sensuality, Carmilla was a scandalous bestseller. To my liking, this is the point at which the horror novel is almost formed. It still has its roots in romanticism rather than terror, but we've now got sex, violence, shock, gore and the whole package is starting to feel like a genuine entertainment product.

Of course, king of the vampire novels is Dracula (1897) by Bram Stoker. Published twenty six years after Carmilla, what makes Dracula interesting is it isn't a vampire story as much as it's a serial-killer story. Stoker was writing during the time of Jack the Ripper, whose Shoreditch killing spree began in 1888. At the time, people were forming vigilante groups to hunt the ripper, a killer whose crimes and invisibility seemed almost supernatural. It's easy to see where Stoker took his inspiration for a group of people setting out to track and kill the Transylvanian Count. Dracula is where it all comes together for the first time; it has the fantasy elements, the romanticism of the gothic period, the shock, horror and blood letting whilst capturing the essence of its time.

Seeing how Dracula was effectively Jack the Ripper brings us to an interesting realisation about horror. With The Monk, the reality of death and mutilation in France seeped into the literature. With Frankenstein, the reality of grave robbing doctors seeped into the writing and with Dracula, the reality of a serial killer made it to the printed page. Throughout history the horror genre has shown an ability to capture the fear of its day and lock it in a time capsule. This is a tradition that continues in the best that we see from horror today. It's especially noticeable in film. Dawn of the Dead captures the consumerism of the 1970's, challenging the idea that you could buy your way to happiness. Watch Cronenberg's The Fly and try not to view it as anything other than the fear of AIDS in the 1980's.The remake of The Hills Have Eyes presented a post 9/11 America and told the story of how Americans had become lost in the desert, surrounded on all sides by people wanting to kill them. The most recent film to capture the zeitgeist is Halloween (the 2018 version) which tapped into the "Me Too" movement by showing how an act of violence decades earlier had permeated through three generations of women. No other genre has the ability to capture social anxiety as profoundly as horror.

In books, what we enjoy now was shaped by writers hundreds of years ago. What we enjoy today is the grown up bastard child of The Castle of Otranto, The Monk, Frankenstein, Carmilla and Dracula. These are the works that led on to the likes of Dennis Wheatley whose occult and supernatural novels such as The Devil Rides Out (1934) formed the basis for many Hammer Horror films. Wheatley wrote books that a modern reader would recognise as a horror novel and they were the first books to be produced using the newly emerging technology of the mass-market paperback. Prior to this time, books were hardback and expensive, but Wheatley's paperbacks, with their garish covers, were designed to thrill and excite. Whilst Lovecraft and Poe treated their novellas and short stories with seriousness, Wheatley was up for fun and mischief, with characters like The Duke de Richleau, a supernatural James Bond using white magic to battle the devil. Wheatley was amongst the first to see his mass-produced paperbacks crossover to cinema and it's easy to trace a line from Wheatley back thirty years to Dracula, then back to Frankenstein and so on.

If there is a thought to take away from this history lesson, it's perhaps a recognition that horror isn't treated as fairly as other genres. In this essay I present two hundred and fifty years of literary history, yet horror is still unworthy of academia. Critics and historians comfortably talk about gothic authors like Charles Dickens, but Dickens might not have written about the ghosts of Christmas if Walpole hadn't made it acceptable with The Castle of Otranto. There is a wealth of history to the horror genre just as worthy of critical debate and discussion as the romantics, yet it's largely neglected. In a way I quite like this. I do enjoy that film critics deride movies like The Texas Chainsaw Massacre or A Nightmare on Elm Street, then slowly change their mind and figure out these stories are culturally important thirty years later. I like that Stephen King was knocking out "trash" for years only to be honored at The White House and pick up a National Medal of Arts; you know instinctively that the awards committee are honoring the staying power of King classics like The Shining and Carrie, yet haven't read anything he's written recently. Generally, film and book critics tend to be decades behind the times when it comes to horror.

In the last few decades, there was a tragic decline in horror publishing and even more so in science-fiction publishing. As the great Sci-Fi writers of yesteryear, such as Arthur C. Clarke and Isaac Asimov died; the publishing industry didn't replace them. So too, the old horror writers were left unrenewed. We found ourselves in a world where a visit to the horror shelf of the bookstore contained Stephen King novels from forty years ago. Carrie, Christine, The Shining and Salem's Lot were still on the shelves, but only a tiny handful of contemporary horror writers made it through the commercial publishing filter.

But whilst things looked bleak from the commercial side, technology opened up an untamed and adventurous landscape. E-books and Print on

Demand books mean there is no longer such a thing as an 'unpublished author'. Those who like horror can write it themselves and get to market without barriers to entry. The gatekeepers to publishing have been replaced and now the limits are only our imagination. There has never been a better time to be an indie horror writer. The future is ours to shape as we wish.

A Dangerous Passage
By
Russell R. James

From the riverbank, you can see a wonderful place, just across the rushing water. A beautiful meadow of green grass stretches up a hillside to a splendid gazebo. A sumptuous picnic is laid out on a table in the center. Seated around it are Stephen King, Ramsey Campbell, and Dean Koontz. A sign atop the gazebo reads HORROR WRITER HEAVEN. They wave to you and beckon you over.

There's a bridge across the river named Traditional Publishing. But Dorothy had an easier time getting to see the Wizard of Oz than you will trying to cross that bridge. The guards there want you to have an agent, and have that agent be on their exclusive list. Then you will need to show your contract with one of the big publishing firms. Special connections in the literary world, or better yet, familial connections may gain you passage. But even with all those tickets punched, there's already a line several miles long of people trying to cross that bridge, with more people joining it every minute.

You either decide that bridge is not for you, or you've already been waiting in the bridge queue for what seems like forever. You opt to just skip it and cross the river. Wet people are not welcomed into the gazebo picnic, but that's not going to be a problem. There are logs floating down the river. All you need to do is hop on one, then hop to the next one, and in no time, you'll be munching on a ham sandwich with one of your literary heroes.

Crossing the river is called the Indie Horror Writer route. Those logs are the opportunities that arise which may have the potential to propel your career forward. Some examples would be a meeting with someone influential, a short story sale, a novel sale, a blog interview, a collaborative venture with another respected author, a position on a panel at a con, or a bookstore signing. There are dozens of other events small and large that could move you closer to that verdant, opposite shore. You know all it will take is that one big log and you'll be home-free.

When one of those logs float close enough, you jump for it. You land and balance without getting wet. Victory!

Sometimes.

More often, it isn't. These floating logs tend to bob and roll. Small presses rise and fall like ocean waves. Editors get fired or move to other presses. Agents quit the business. Your writing collaborator has a family emergency and that project fizzles. I've been on panels at cons with tens of thousands of attendees, but under five attend the panel. The fact that all these venues and opportunities are relatively small means that single, unplanned events are very disruptive for them.

Then even if you do land on a big stable log, you have no control over the river's current. You may be the best werewolf storyteller ever born, but after Hollywood cranks out three werewolf films in nine months, the public appetite for lycanthropy has been satiated, and your magnum opus may have no takers.

I'm not telling you this parable to depress you, but to remind you of something. If you are going to take this indie route, you need one quality more important than writing skill or creativity. You need optimism. In your heart, you must believe that no matter how wobbly and waterlogged your current log is, the perfect one is about to float by, and you're ready to jump for it.

This book is full of anecdotes and examples of authors leaping between those logs, and some of those stories might be sad. But they are also inspirational, because that author is still here to write them. That writer hasn't given up because they still know that exceptional log is about to float downstream.

An amazing collection of indie authors are about to gather around the campfire, dry their wet clothes, and tell you their stories. Pull up a camp chair, listen, and learn.

12 Point, Times New Roman
By
David Moody

I hope you don't mind, but I'm going to start this with a (very brief) history lesson. It'll help put things in context.

My first novel was published traditionally back in 1996. It sank without a trace. When it came to releasing a follow-up a few years later, the only thing I knew for certain was that I didn't want to repeat my earlier mistakes and climb straight back onto the same submission-rejection merry-go-round again. Second time around, I wanted more control. I'd already accepted that book #2 (AUTUMN) probably wasn't going to make me famous, but I was determined to get it in front of as many potential readers as possible. What good's an author without readers, I thought? I decided to give the book away to anyone who wanted it, and it's no exaggeration to say that decision changed my life.

I was very fortunate in that, by chance, I unexpectedly hit the crest of three waves with that release. First, during the period I made AUTUMN available free online, the eBook market came into existence and then exploded. Second, I was taking my first tentative steps onto the internet during its formative years, and free eBook promotions were pretty much unheard of. Only a handful of folks were giving their fiction away, and yet there was a huge untapped audience waiting to read it. Third, I was writing about zombies when hardly anyone else was. And pretty much at the same time as I released AUTUMN into the world, 28 DAYS LATER and then the DAWN OF THE DEAD remake hit the screens, and THE WALKING DEAD first appeared in print. It was all down to luck more than judgement, but my timing couldn't have been much better.

Long story short, AUTUMN was downloaded by a lot of people in a relatively short period of time, exceeding my wildest expectations. It went on to spawn a series of sequels (I'm now up to nine books), and a movie which starred David Carradine (KILL BILL) in one of his final roles. The film rights to another one of my books, HATER, were optioned by Guillermo del Toro and, as a result, publishing rights to the HATER and AUTUMN books were picked up by St Martin's Press in New York and subsequently sold around the world.

So, why am I telling you this? It's not to boast or to gloat, that much is for sure. I'm convinced people gave my books a shot because they looked the part. It wasn't always that way, though, and I want to share some of the most important publishing tips that I've picked up over the last twenty-something years. I learnt a lot through trial and error when I first started out, and then, when I got to work with major publishing houses, I learnt a heck of a lot more that I've since been able to apply to my independent releases.

First things first — notice that I call it 'independent' publishing? I think that's an important distinction. Back when I started out, self-publishing was a dirty secret you didn't dare admit to. Very few people were doing it, and those who were, were often making a hash of it. Crappy covers, unedited content, errors galore . . . every publisher's nightmare. The term 'self-publishing' still conjures up memories of those early nightmares. My ethos was to try to publish books that were indistinguishable in look and feel from those put out by major publishing houses. It's taken a long time for the indie scene to catch up, but I think we're finally able to do that (with all but a few caveats).

Whether you publish your own books independently, or you release the work of other writers and creatives, you're not pretending to be a publisher, you ARE a publisher. What you do might not be on the scale of those huge New York or London based publishing houses, but you need to understand that you are fulfilling many of the same functions as those companies, and you have the right to be called a publisher too. What you do with that right, however, is up to you. The more exacting and professional you are, the less obvious the distinction between you and the majors will become. When a reader holds a book in their hands (or loads it onto their Kindle or pipes it through their headphones), they couldn't give a damn how many people work for the company that's behind it. It could have taken an army of editors, designers, publicists, and whoever to get it to them, or it might have just been one grumpy old bugger working from his home office in Birmingham (ie, me). It doesn't matter – provided the book meets their expectations (physically, I mean), then they likely won't give its production a second thought.

They'll realise soon enough if you don't get it right, though.

I don't know about you, but I hate it when I'm snatched out of a story. Have you ever been watching a film only for a boom mic to drop into view or a camera operator's reflection to appear in a mirror? You're immediately reminded that you're watching a movie, and that you're one step removed from the events on screen. I think the same happens in books when readers find typos, glaring errors, or other inconsistencies. It might sound like I'm being overly pedantic here, but I'm really not. I have no idea how Guillermo del Toro ended up with a copy of my independently published edition of HATER on his desk. It had only been out for around 6 months and had sold less than 1000 copies when I first had contact with Hollywood. Regardless, I genuinely believe that if HATER hadn't looked as if it had been professionally published, if I hadn't taken as much care with the formatting, the edit, and the design of the book as I did with the story itself, no one would have given it the time of day.

These days, we're fortunate to be able to tap into vast online marketplaces with relative ease, and to use eBook, audiobook, and print-on-demand technologies to get our books in front of the eyes (and ears) of huge numbers of readers. Competition, however, is fiercer than ever, and you might only get one chance to impress. A great story told with style is obviously the key ingredient to success – without that you're screwed – but there's every chance you'll lose scores of potential readers if your book doesn't look the part.

I recommend coming up with a brand to help prolong the illusion. Apologies if I'm sounding a little too corporate. I come from a finance operations and customer service background, and whilst telling great stories is the most important thing to me as a writer, as a publisher I sometimes find it hard to drop all the corporate bullshit.

My brand is Infected Books. I started the business in 2001 when AUTUMN first started to gain traction. The difference it made having a named publisher behind the book was remarkable (even if it was a name I came up with and was hiding behind). As I've said, I realised pretty much straightaway how important it was to try and look like one of the big boys. The IB name helped, but it still took many more years and a number of misfires and silly mistakes to fully understand what I needed to do.

The first AUTUMN eBook was a Word file. Seriously. And in terms of formatting . . . other than centred titles and chapter headings, there pretty much wasn't any. Everything was 12 point, Times New Roman. I got away with it because we were all in the dark back in the early days – indie publishers and readers alike – and enough people were willing to give me a chance. If I was starting out today, I wouldn't have got a look in. The first cover I designed was a photograph pinched off a website that I'd blurred, reversed, and turned greyscale, then slapped the name of the book over the top in a particularly ugly font. It was awful. The next version wasn't much better – I had some decent artwork at last, but I hadn't yet learnt the peculiarities of formatting an image for print and the quirks of colour profiles, so all the edits I'd made that were invisible on my knackered old computer screen, were glaringly obvious in paperback. And yes, those early print-on-demand paperbacks were also set in Times New Roman!

In my defence, though, in those very early days, nothing was straightforward. Over the following years, as the technology advanced, I learnt a lot about book production through trial and error. The real turning point for me came when I was working with Gollancz on the UK re-releases of AUTUMN and HATER and the publication of their various sequels. When it came to the fifth AUTUMN book – AFTERMATH – the Gollancz team told me it was no longer cost-effective for them to produce a hardcover edition. A lot of readers were disappointed because they'd got the rest of the series in hardcover and wanted to complete the set. I re-launched Infected Books, and I was able to reach an agreement with my editor to publish a hardcover edition through IB in collaboration with Gollancz.

Their hardcover had already been designed, and they were generous enough to allow me to use and adapt their interior and cover files. I 'reverse-engineered' them so that I could properly understand how a traditional publisher formats a book, and I've applied my findings to every paperback and hardcover I've released in the ten years or so since.

By the way, I'd recommend doing this yourself. Although you're unlikely to have access to the digital files, why not take a book off your shelf that has an interior you particularly like the look of and take some time trying to understand what it is you like about it. Use a ruler to measure the area of the text, look at the formatting of chapter headings, investigate how they've formatted their front matter and any additional material about the author etc. You might think this is over the top, but in my experience it's well worth your time.

Here are some of the other key things I've learnt that you might find useful . . .

Keep track of your cast

If you're writing a book (or books) with a large cast of characters, you need to keep track of them. Some publishers produce a Dramatis Personae (cast of characters) and I recommend you do the same. It doesn't have to be anything fancy – just a separate document with a list of people's names, followed by any important information that's pertinent to the story (Are they still alive? Have they been injured? How did you kill them? and so on). This might sound over-the-top, but I did manage to have a character appear in two locations simultaneously in one of the early AUTUMN books, and in a late draft of ALL ROADS END HERE, the penultimate HATER novel, I somehow managed to include a reference to a character I'd deleted after the very first draft! I've recently written a standalone trilogy of AUTUMN novels with a very large cast (DAWN, INFERNO, and EXODUS). To keep track of the exploits of more than sixty characters across three novels, my dramatis personae ended up being a ridiculously complicated spreadsheet, but it did the trick.

Watch out for your current quirks.

I'm not an editor, and this is not intended to be a guide to editing, but there is one thing I'd like to share because even now, more than twenty books in, it's something I'm still guilty of. As I'm writing each book, I seem to develop a particular quirk of language that I'll use again and again. The first time it was brought to my attention, it was shoulder shrugging. At least one character in almost every conversation I wrote in the original version of AUTUMN would shrug their shoulders. I'd been oblivious when I'd written the book, but as soon as it was pointed out to me, it was painfully obvious. In STRANGERS, I'd become addicted to using ellipses . . . Even as recently as the last but one AUTUMN novel, INFERNO, I'd fallen into the trap of describing the scale of things multiple times – there were thousands upon thousands upon thousands of corpses, they walked mile upon mile upon mile, it happened again and again and again etc. The reason I'm raising this, is that if your editor points out that you've developed a current quirk, you should 'find and replace' the troublesome phrase throughout your manuscript and get rid of it. You'll be surprised how easy it is to fall into the trap, and you'll be equally surprised how much better your book will read once you've exorcised it.

Keep track of your versions

I don't know about you, but I tend to release paperback, hardcover, eBook, and audiobook versions of most of my books. Once I've got the final text back from my editor, I start working on all those individual formats. It's important to keep your files organised so that if you make a change to one, you can quickly make the same changes on all the others, and also so you know you're always working on the most up-to-date file. Feel free to stop reading and fall asleep at this point if you like, but I like to keep a single main folder for each book, with subfolders inside named Writing and Production. In the Production folder, I have further subfolders for Print (split into Hardcover and Paperback as necessary), as well as Audio and eBook. The only files in each of those subfolders are the book content and the finished artwork. If I find a typo in the manuscript, I know exactly what files need updating. Everything else gets shifted to the archives so I don't end up using the wrong thing.

Keep track of your look

I have another folder where I keep specific elements that I know I'll use time and time again when I'm publishing books. My company logos, the format I use for my front matter, the format and wording I use for the back matter – my 'About the Author' page and a list of my books. Also, to make sure I have a consistent look across my titles (particularly across a series), I keep a list of the technical details such as:

- The fonts – size, weight, font family etc

- eBook templates
- How chapter and section headings are formatted, the use of drop caps etc
- The page dimensions, margin size, character and line spacing
- Spread dimensions (the margins on right and left facing pages will be different)
- Numbers! Look closely and you'll see that some publishers use a different font for any numbers in the body of a book (I use Sabon RomanSC if you're interested!)

The final countdown

I have a final proofing checklist that I go back to. Microsoft Word has a habit of making annoying autocorrections – replacing dashes with lines, converting certain character combinations to other characters (or even emojis!) that this helps to spot. I've found a checklist invaluable for catching certain errors that might otherwise go overlooked:

- Make sure all your text is there. This may sound obvious, but if you've imported a file from your word processor into whatever program you use to format your print book or your ebook, make sure it's all imported properly
- Hyphenation – make sure the use of hyphens and em dashes (and the spacing

around them) is standardised across your text

- Check scene breaks – I use a line space between paragraphs to indicate a scene change in print, with a single asterisk at the start or end of a page if that's where the break occurs. In eBooks, every scene break is marked with a symbol
- Ensure that your tab spacing is consistent throughout
- Ellipses – check these have formatted correctly and consistently throughout your text
- Quote marks – some publishers use 'single' quotes for speech, some use "double". Whichever you go for, make sure your usage is consistent throughout. Are you using 'smart' quotes? Check that all start and end quotes are as they should be and are pointing the right way
- Make sure your chapters are numbered correctly – sounds obvious, but the editor of one of my traditionally published books split the manuscript in half to make it easier for her to work on. It was only when we were doing the final copy-edit before going to print and I was checking the chapter headings that we realised an entire

chapter right in the middle of the book had got lost along the way

- Similarly, check your page numbers are sequential
- Check your chapters are formatted correctly – I start chapters about a quarter of the way down a page. In special hardcovers, I'll only start new chapters on facing pages. It's important that all chapters are formatted the same.
- Make sure you've updated your front matter – the copyright notice needs to be up-to-date, and you'll need to ensure the right ISBN is quoted.

I know this must all sound very pedantic, and I'm sure you do most if not all of this anyway, but this stuff really does matter. If one of my independently published books can end up in Guillermo del Toro's hands, there's no reason why one of yours can't too.

Ultimately, as an author, every single reader is equally important to me. Whether they're your most slavish fan who buys everything you write, or if they picked your book up from a second-hand store because they liked the cover, every person's opinion matters. Regardless of how much you spend on marketing each year, and how many in-person events you attend or podcasts you guest on, the quality of your books will always be your best advert. Make sure you get it right. Reader goodwill is fragile: it's hard to earn, and you can lose it in a heartbeat.

Back When I Was a Kid....
By
John Everson

Next year (2024) will mark my 30th year as a published horror author. Given that my first short story appeared in January 1994, I guess *this* year marks my 30th year as an active author submitting pieces to magazines and anthologies. Somehow... I guess I'm now part of the "old guard" of horror.

When I first started out, there was no real Internet. The World Wide Web began in the early '90s, so websites were rare and rudimentary at best. Back then, if you wanted to submit a story to a magazine, you had to print it out, put it in an envelope with a cover letter, add a self-addressed stamped envelope so the editor could send you their reply, and then drop it at the post office and wait weeks or months to hear back. In the early to mid-90s, I used to write a short story just about every other weekend, send each of them off to a handful of publications, and then... watch the mail for acceptances and rejections every day.

At my prime, I had a couple dozen stories in circulation that I was waiting for responses on at any one time. And man, did I used to wait anxiously for responses! Back then, I'd call my wife every day from work to check in (no texts or very much email use then!) and I always asked: did I get any mail?

One of my early short horror stories was inspired by that anxiousness and called "Waiting for the Mail."

Back then, there were also dozens and dozens of small "zines" that people printed at the local copy shop (many of them hand-stapled in their basements). Many only had 50-100 subscribers and finding out about them was a challenge all by itself. I used to go to Borders and Barnes & Noble bookstores all the time and look at the back pages of the *Writers Market* magazine to see if there were any ads for new zines to submit to. And now and then, a new literary magazine friendly to horror also appeared on their magazine shelves. I'd buy those, read them to get a feel for what they were about and see if I had any stories that would fit the market.

With each new magazine you discovered as a writer, you got connected to another small community of horror fans, and those usually mentioned other venues… so your net expanded. And there was a magazine that basically all small press indie authors subscribed to – Janet Fox's

Scavenger's Newsletter. It listed new and open magazine and anthology markets each month, with descriptions of what the editors were looking for and what they paid. *Scav* was the mainline of the horror community.

The other mainline was... The World Horror Convention. Started in 1991, it was put on each spring in a different city by different local host committees. I started attending in 2000, when my first collection of fiction, *Cage of Bones & Other Deadly Obsessions* was gearing up for release. And that... was an eye-opener. Suddenly I met all of these people I'd corresponded with for years on paper (and eventually email). And you know what? They were NICE!

That's the one thing that I've always thought about the horror community. There are so many genuinely nice, well-meaning people in the group. People often have the assumption that people who write bone-grinding, violent, extreme horror tales are going to be pretty edgy themselves... but I found that was generally not the case at all. Gruesome tattoos and wild hair aside, some of the people who wrote the darkest things were actually the most sensitive souls of all.

I went to the WHC every year for the next decade. It was the highlight of my years in the 2000s – that weekend where I got to relax, be myself and actually talk face-to-face with people who were *like* me. I looked forward to hanging out and grabbing dinners with people like Edward Lee and Gerard Houarner and Mehitobel Wilson and Loren Rhoads and some amazing people (my core friends, honestly) who are not with us anymore – Dave Barnett, Charlee Jacob and GAK. I met Richard Laymon and Richard Matheson and William F. Nolan and Peter Straub, also all gone now. It was really an amazing time to be a writer. The intersection of the classic horror names of the '80s with the modern breed who were making their marks on a new era.

But in some ways, it was a much lonelier time. Horror writers often find that their family and "normal" friends and workmates are not terribly sympathetic to their love of the macabre. That was why I loved the World Horror Convention so deeply. It was the one time of year that I could actually talk about the things I loved with people who understood.

The early web helped... people congregated in "chat rooms" on AOL, CompuServe and GEnie and eventually, message board constructs like

Shocklines. The downside was that the age of the flame war began, as people learned that you could hide behind anonymity and say whatever you wanted without repercussion. It didn't bring out the best in people in general and horror folk were no exception. But that was the early stage... with the growth of social media networks like MySpace and then Facebook and Twitter and then Instagram and now TikTok... a whole new style of connection evolved.

Now you could chat up writers and editors on instant messages at any time of the day or night. People moved outside of the cliquey message board constructs... and circles of friends and alliances expanded at an astonishing rate. In 20 years, we went from only being able to talk to fellow horror writers and fans once or twice a year, to making hundreds and thousands of like-minded friends online.

I'll be honest, I don't know that it's all for the better. But what I do know is that horror folk still tend to be some pretty nice, helpful souls. We're all in this because we love the offbeat, the not-quite-ready-for-prime-time. We like it dark and nasty and maybe not the kind of thing you can fist-pump about at the corporate watercooler. That shared love of the strange binds us, and means that other members of the "tribe" are always ready to help.

When I started out, I worked exclusively in the small indie press. People celebrated each other and did whatever they could to help. They volunteered to edit, to design covers, to help with marketing. I used to copy edit for Necro, Delirium, Earthling and Cemetery Dance, often simply being paid in hardcover books. It was kind of like being in a club – you all pitched in to make things better. Eventually, I sold books to the mass market (Leisure Books), and I wasn't quite so "indie" anymore. I got too busy to copyedit other people's novels or design websites for publishers and authors I liked. I've never left the indie scene behind, but over the past few years, I have been less involved as Flame Tree Press marketed my books and I raised a high schooler.

When I found myself with a truly independent release again this year with *The Night Mother*, a sequel to my Bram Stoker Award nominee *NightWhere*, it was a time of reconnecting to some extent. I had no marketing department or art department behind me for the first time in years... And so I reached out, via old email addresses and Facebook IMs to see if there were still "friendly" horror fans and editors and reviewers out there, like there used to be.

There were.

The names and faces have changed, but the spirit remains. We all still want horror to transcend. I reached out to reviewers and fellow authors to see if they would help me to get the word out about the new novel. I found a lot of the people who were part of the community five or six years ago were gone now… but those who have taken their place are just as supportive. They helped me choose new cover art and pointed me towards outlets where I could get the new novel some review play.

Maybe it's because we fear the dark more than most, and confront it on the page whenever we write. Maybe it's because we spend so much time alone, wrestling with word choice, bending language to provide the reader with just a hint of the horrible things we imagine. For whatever reason, horror writers – the indie horror community – are generally supportive of each other. If you're cool to them… they'll pitch in to help you when you need it.

A lot has changed over the past 30 years… hell, just about everything. But one thing has remained the same. Horror writers strike fear on a daily basis in their readers, who thirst for the adrenaline rush a good scare can bring. And ironically, horror writers really are actually...

...Nice!

Living the Pipe Dream
By
Brian Moreland

My journey to becoming a horror author began in early childhood in the 1970s. I made up stories while playing with toy soldiers that battled rubber monsters. As a horror movie buff, I watched creature features like *Food of the Gods*, *Godzilla*, and *Snowbeast* every Saturday on TV. I loved the classic Universal monsters: Dracula, Wolf Man, Frankenstein and the Creature from the Black Lagoon. Weeknights, I watched episodes of *The Twilight Zone* and *Outer Limits*. In my bedroom, I read horror comics and movie magazines like *Famous Monsters of Film Land* and *Fangoria*. What I enjoyed most was going to the movie theater. Seeing *Alien*, *Halloween*, and *A Nightmare on Elm Street* on the big screen thrilled and terrified me. The arrival of cable TV delivered *John Carpenter's The Thing* and *Creepshow* into my living room. The invention of VHS brought in the motherlode of horror movie choices. Among my favorites were the original *Evil Dead* and Argento's and Bava's *Demons*. It was a blast growing up as a teenager in the 1980s.

Monsters were with me throughout my grade school years. Back then, I had no idea I was destined to become a writer of scary stories. It wasn't until high school that I discovered the joy of reading horror fiction. My first foray into chilling prose that got under my skin was from reading Edgar Alle Poe. I read every short story in Stephen King's *Night Shift*. Then I devoured all three volumes of Clive Barker's *Books of Blood*. Some stories, like "The Midnight Meat Train," stayed with me long after. There was something about horror fiction that seemed to touch me deeper. It's such a fun genre. Anything can happen in a horror story. There's room to explore every kind of monster from the humankind to evil spirits in haunted houses. From vampires, werewolves and zombies to cosmic Lovecraftian creatures from other dimensions.

I attended the University of Texas at Austin from 1987-1992. My freshman year I advanced from reading short stories to novels. Like most horror readers, I read a lot of Stephen King. I also discovered a love for early Dean Koontz, James Herbert, and Robert McCammon. Spring semester my freshman year, I challenged myself to write a horror novel. I skipped many classes and wrote for hours and days on end. I didn't own a computer, so I wrote at the school's computer lab on these old IBMs with black screens and green words. Within a few months, I completed a first draft of what, many drafts and years later, would become *The Devil's Woods*.

I was so proud of my first manuscript, I had it bound with a black hard cover. For the first time in my life, at the age of 19, I knew what I wanted to be when I grew up: a horror novelist. I've always been a big dreamer and especially so during my college years, when my whole adult life was still ahead of me. My pipe dream was to have an accomplished career like Stephen King and Clive Barker. I aspired to write dozens of bestselling novels with kickass covers. I imagined seeing my stories made into popular horror movies. In this fantasy career, I would never have to work a regular job because six-figure royalty checks would constantly fill my mailbox. Publishers would accept every book or short story I submitted. And my books would always be available to readers at bookstores.

Then came adulthood. Stark realities of the publishing business popped my dream career balloon again and again. Throughout my twenties and thirties, I wrote numerous short story and novel manuscripts. Then with fingers crossed, I played the query and submissions game. I received countless rejection letters from literary agents and editors. One agent told me I had some talent and encouraged me to keep developing my craft. Taking that to heart, I read numerous books on the mechanics of writing fiction and took some writing workshops. I steadily improved and found my voice.

While I stood on the sidelines through the 1990s and early 2000s, I watched the horror publishing industry crash and bounce back and continuously evolve. After years of failing to land an agent or publisher, I decided to jump-start my career on my own. So, I self-published my first novel, *Shadows in the Mist*. Wearing my "publisher" hat, I did everything from hiring an editor and book designers to self-promoting to hustling my books at horror conventions. My World War II horror novel sold well and won an IPPY gold medal for Best Horror Novel, which I received in New York. My author career was finally happening in the world outside of my head.

Through that first novel's success, I landed a literary agent, and she sold *Shadows in the Mist* to Berkley-Penguin for a mass paperback deal. At last, I achieved one of my major goals: a traditional publishing deal with a major publisher. I was elated when I received my first advance check. My joy sky-rocketed to the moon when the small paperback version of *Shadows in the Mist* appeared on the shelves of bookstores. My career lifted off the ground.

I kept writing manuscripts. Some I abandoned and some I finished and submitted. I strived to continuously grow as a writer. I joined a writer's group where I read a few chapters of my current book. The feedback I received over the years has been priceless. I learned my strengths and weaknesses and how to take criticism. My writers group also challenged me to write, revise, and edit my manuscripts until they were good enough to be published.

From 2011-2017, I published several novels and novellas through a mid-sized publisher, Samhain Publishing, and got to work with an amazing editor, Don D'Auria. His encouragement inspired me to keep writing more books. As a Samhain author, I attended horror cons and signed books alongside many talented authors, some of them my personal heroes. The fun ride eventually ended when Samhain closed its doors and reverted the rights to my books back to me. This happened at the same time that my audio publisher closed its doors.

Suddenly overnight, I went from several books available through booksellers and earning royalties to no published books and zero earnings. Like a train hitting the breaks, my career stalled. A dark period followed. By this time, I was on the cusp of turning 50. I had already suffered through ups and downs in the horror business and endured publishing droughts. I struggled to tap into that enthusiasm for working as a professional novelist that I had felt in my youth.

My younger self had never dreamed that there would be heart-breaking downturns during my career, that publishers would fold their business, that earnings would fall flat, that I would go through periods of writer's block, or that after some success I'd still receive rejections. On top of the disappointments that can happen during a writer's career, I got sidetracked from writing by personal disruptions in my life. Some years, I put aside writing projects to work jobs that covered living expenses. Many times, I considered quitting writing fiction altogether. Then I'd hear the advice bestselling author Robert Crais once gave me at a book signing: "Never give up." From time to time, I'd remind myself that *stories matter*. The world needs us writers to write stories, even scary ones with monsters.

Even through those dark times of career uncertainty, I continued to write new fiction: short stories, novellas, chapters for novels. I write horror because I'm a diehard fan of the genre. I enjoy inventing stories, characters, monsters, and imaginary worlds. I love entertaining readers and meeting fellow booklovers. I've learned that with persistence, tenacity, and writing new manuscripts, that success can happen along the way. Your stories can sell, get published, and get discovered by readers who love them.

The dark times eventually turned bright again. I continue to sell more short stories, novellas, and novels to new publishers. It remains to be seen whether I will achieve all the grand goals I had envisioned in my youth. My writer's journey is still unfolding. I now know with conviction that I will never give up writing. I will always search within my soul for that next story to bring to life and share with the world. Whether I experience highs or lows along my writer's journey, I'll continue living the pipe dream.

Developing Your Writing Process
By
Tom Deady

When I was an aspiring writer, devouring every "how to" book I could get my hands on and attending workshops and conventions on the craft, there was one piece of advice that I heard almost unanimously: Writers must write every day. I'm here to tell you it's the worst advice I've ever received.

Writing is like exercise. If you were new to running, there isn't a coach in the world who would advise you to run every day. It's overwhelming, and a lot of unnecessary pressure. Inevitably, when you miss a day — and you will miss a day — you become discouraged. You feel like you've failed. And sometimes, you give up.

Writing, (like running) is hard. It's exhausting. It's a solitary experience that can't be easily measured to show success. Most people starting out are juggling numerous other responsibilities. Work, school, family…and those all take priority over writing. There are going to be days that these obligations leave you lacking the creativity to sit down at the keyboard. And that is perfectly acceptable!

My first novel, *Haven*, took me fifteen years to write. I did it in fits and starts while working two jobs, going to night school, and raising two daughters. I would work on it for a while, miss a few days, and shelf the novel because I wasn't writing every day. It had been drilled into my head that writers write every day, so obviously *I wasn't a writer*.

I eventually finished *Haven*. It was published by Cemetery Dance and went on to win the Bram Stoker Award for Superior Achievement in a First Novel. I'm not telling you that to brag, I'm telling you because I don't want you to get discouraged and put your novel on the back burner because you can't write every day.

It takes a long time to get the writing muscle in good enough shape that writing every day is even possible. Yes, I'm going to stick with the exercise analogy. As a runner, some days I drag myself outside, or to the treadmill, and force myself to run a few slow, labored miles. Some days I can't find the mental energy to do it at all. Writing is the same way.

There are going to be days (or nights) when the idea of sitting in front of your keyboard and finding the energy to be creative is simply too much. There are going to be other times when you sit there staring at the blinking cursor and squeeze out a few words, filled with self-loathing and imposter syndrome. Just like the few hard miles that feel so awful, those words might be the most important.

Those difficult times, those hard words forced out at birth kicking and screaming, are how you become a writer. It's that grueling time at the keyboard where you start to develop your writing process.

Yes, writing is a process. But it's a truly unique process, different for everyone. Which makes learning *your* process that much harder. There is no instruction manual, no step-by-step set of instructions that work for everybody. Every writer has their own process that works for them. Yes, from a distance it may be *similar* to others, but upon closer scrutiny it is as different and unique as a snowflake.

It took me years to figure out my writing process. And to be honest, it's still evolving. So now that I've told you a piece of bad advice, I'm going to share something that does work for me. Keeping track of word count.

For years I have been participating in National Novel Writing Month, or NaNoWriMo. It's an annual event with the goal of writing a novel during the month of November. For the sake of the event, a novel is considered fifty thousand words. It's an insane, caffeine-fueled thirty days of self-induced madness. And I love it.

I tried it for the first time in 2014 and wrote the first fifty thousand words of what eventually became my second novel, *Eternal Darkness*. I've attempted it every year since, managing to make the goal more often than not. Even the years I "failed" I still ended up with upwards of thirty thousand words, a lot for me.

It wasn't until 2020, just before the pandemic began, that I discovered why NaNoWriMo always worked for me. That January, I attended a writing retreat, at the Von Trapp Lodge in Vermont. It was a bunch of writers hanging out with no real agenda other than writing. I decided that weekend that I was going to keep track of how much I accomplished. It was my way of seeing how productive I could be if writing was my full-time gig. I think I ended up with about seven thousand words over the three-day weekend.

When I got home, I continued tracking my word count. As the weeks and months went on, it became apparent that the simple act of keeping track of my progress, inspired me not only to keep writing, but to write more. To circle back to the running analogy, everyone wants to improve, beating their fastest time or the longest run. That same competitive drive works (for me at least) in writing.

Once I realized what my average monthly output was, I set that as a goal. I didn't put any pressure on myself to write every day, or even reach a specific number of words on the days I did write. And you know what? I wrote more in 2020 than I ever had before. I dropped off a bit in 2021, mostly because I was in the process of editing a novel, a novella, and a short story collection. In 2022 I bounced back and ended the year with about the same number of words as 2020, and this year I'm on pace to do the same.

You've probably noticed I didn't mention my monthly goals or my annual word count. That's because this is not a competition between you and me. It's a competition between you, all of your other life responsibilities, and your desire to be a writer. There is no right or wrong goal for you to set. As long as you make it realistic and measurable, you can succeed.

There are a lot of other factors that go into your writing process. One is the time of day you write. Some people get up early, before their day job, and write. Others use their lunch break. For me, it was always late at night, after the family went to bed. That is still my most productive time to write.

Where you write is also important. When I was starting out, it was important for me to have a dedicated writing space. Part of it was to get in the writing mindset. For me, routine was very important when I was starting out. You don't need an elaborate wood-paneled office, or a personal library lined with bookshelves. You just need a corner of the world to call your own. It can be a specific seat at the dining room table, or a makeshift set-up in the basement or garage. It doesn't even have to be at home. I did a lot of writing at a local coffee shop, and I know some people who write while riding the commuter train to work every day.

There you have it, my writing process in a neat, five-page article that was thirty years in the making. Take from this what you can use, what you think might work for you, and throw the rest away. Your writing process is going to be a patchwork of ideas that you weave together over the years, just like mine was. I guarantee it won't look exactly like mine, or anybody else's, and that's what makes it yours.

Chase Those Nightmares

By

John Durgin

I may work in finance during the day, but by nightfall, I'm killing monsters. No, I'm not Batman (although I often tell my son I am), I'm a horror writer. It's in my bones, and always has been. So why did it take me until my mid-thirties to even pick up a keyboard and type my first story? I'll tell you why. DOUBT. The lack of a degree in anything to do with writing, literature, etc. Like many creatives, I spent my entire life dreaming of someday telling stories. At one point when I was eight or nine, I'd run through the woods making a movie in my head about a massive anaconda chasing me through the forest. Yes, I'd just watched the movie Anaconda. No, I didn't know what plagiarism was back then. When I settled down from my daily one-man shows, I'd watch every horror movie my parents would let me, read every horror novel I could get my hands on.

Like many kids of the 90's, I started out with Goosebumps. I couldn't wait for the Scholastic flyer to show up every month so I could auto-buy the next in the series. I would fly home and start reading it, well into the night when the blankets would get tossed over my head, flashlight in hand. Then the eighth grade came, and I discovered a copy of *IT* by Stephen King. Never in a million years did I think at that age I could read such a large book. Never mind that I was far too young to consume that sort of content, but things were different in the 90's. So, my origin story clearly isn't the most original. Many authors around my age would probably say the same exact thing for their beginning. R.L. Stine introduced us to horror, Stephen King made us fall in love with it.

I knew from that moment on that my dream was to be a writer. Which brings me back to my original question: Why did I wait until age thirty-six to write my first ever story? There is no hidden treasure chest of rejected manuscripts. No cute third-grade stories I wrote about my dog falling in toxic waste and becoming a rabid werewolf. I went my whole life just keeping that dream locked inside. I took film classes in high school and found my core group of friends who obsessed over horror movies just as much as I did. Anyone who's read *The Cursed Among Us*, I can tell you that the group of friends in the book WAS my group of friends growing up. We made horror movies in the woods; we wrote shitty movie scripts. But that was the extent of it for me. I never took it seriously enough at a young age to sit down and write when the creative itch was there.

My college years arrived, and I went to school for Business Management—a far cry from anything creative. And then I read *On Writing: A Memoir of the Craft,* by Stephen King, finding out he basically came out of the womb writing stories. My hero had been doing it since the time he was in diapers, and here I was in my twenties without ever pursuing it. When that should have motivated me even more, it instead deflated my hopes. I'd missed too much time, hadn't put in the practice to master the craft. I started a career in finance and had kids. Bills, responsibilities, and life got in the way of even thinking about my dreams. There were a few late-night, drunken conversations with my wife where I confessed that I dreamed of being a horror author, and while I know my day job pays well and supports our family, writing is what I always found myself most passionate about. In her defense, she told me to try it. What was there to lose? But I didn't listen. I was too afraid of failure and felt stupid for even thinking I stood a chance at this gig.

Fast-forward more than fifteen years later to the pandemic. With nowhere to go, nobody to see, there was a hell of a lot more time on my hands. I took a long look in the mirror and told myself if it wasn't going to happen now, it never would. I had no more excuses. I got back into art, spending some of my free time during the pandemic drawing and opening an Etsy shop. That led to co-founding Livid Comics, where I wrote professionally for the first time in my life, albeit not in prose form. Writing comics gave me even more of an itch to attempt prose, so I wrote my first ever short story, titled "A Walk on the Beach." After submitting it to two anthologies and not hearing back for a bit, I assumed it wasn't good enough and focused on the comic stuff some more. Then something happened... it got accepted. By *both* anthologies. To say I was speechless would be an understatement. While this story was far from my best work, it was good enough to get into two books, and motivated me to try my hand at a novella. That novella turned into a novel, my debut *The Cursed Among Us*, which went on to become an Amazon bestseller and #1 new release, and made the Bram Stoker preliminary ballot for the First Novel category.

The reason I tell you all this is for two reasons. First, don't ever feel like you aren't good enough, that you don't stand a chance in this crazy world of make believe. I doubted myself so long, as I know so many aspiring writers do. If you don't believe in yourself, you will either never put those words on paper, or if you do somehow get them written but still don't believe, everyone will know that when they read your work. Secondly, I wanted to show you it IS possible. There are plenty of writers I could list who are very successful and never went to college. It's important to know that because imposter syndrome is a real bitch. But I also came here to give some advice on things that worked for me. While I can't guarantee it will work for everyone, hell it may not even work for me on my next book, I took a very methodical approach to putting a book into the world. Give it a shot. Like my wife said, what do you have to lose?

10 STEPS TO TAKE WHEN SELF-PUBLISHING

1. It all starts with networking. Talk with as many authors and readers as possible early on, well before the book is done. Join Facebook groups, follow and interact on Twitter and TikTok, be active about others' work and celebrate your love of horror together. Pick their brains, most of us love helping others succeed and paying it forward. This is a give-and-take industry, but don't go into it expecting to "take" just because you "give." Give because you want to and enjoy supporting authors you like.

2. I have a wife and two kids, plus a day job. So, I get that it can be impossible to write every single day. Don't beat yourself up if you miss a day here and there—but write every single chance you get. I've written three books this past year, all with

twenty-minute blocks here, or an hour there. If I have free time, I'm either writing or reading. Personally, I don't give myself a wordcount goal each day, because I don't want to put that sort of pressure on myself. I just have fun and tell the story I want to tell. Some days that may lead to a few thousand words, others it might only be five hundred words. You have to try and not allow the idea of writing a novel to fester in your mind as some daunting task. I wrote my first two novels in about three months each, doing it mostly in small writing blocks.

3. No matter what, finish that first draft! Typing the words "The End" is one of the best feelings in the world. And as others have pointed out to me on my journey, you can't edit what you don't write. The second and third drafts are for tightening up plot holes and making it sound all pretty.

4. Seek out beta readers, especially early on in your career. There are many groups online that have readers ready to gobble up books to help give their input. The Books of Horror Freeview group on Facebook is full of beta/ARC readers.

5. If you plan to self-publish, be sure not to cheap out on two things—a cover artist and an editor. These two things can make or break your success. When nobody knows your name, think of how crucial it is to put a book out with an eye-popping cover. I get that many young writers can't afford a pricy cover, but many of today's top cover artists on the Indie scene are willing to work with writers. Whether it be payment plans, or even offering their pre-made covers at a discount, it is so important. And then there's an editor. Be sure you are not getting taken advantage of. There are some that smell blood with the newbies and move in like sharks trying to make a few extra bucks. Ask around. Many of us are happy to refer you to a great editor that won't break the bank. What you don't want to do is put months into getting a book ready, get a killer cover, and then skimp on the editing and have it destroyed in reviews.

6. Once you have edited the book, you have to format it before sending it off to early readers and getting some of those early nerve-wracking reviews. Formatting. I didn't even know what formatting was when I started this journey. If you aren't comfortable doing it yourself, ask around and you will find some affordable formatters. These are the people who get the book interior ready for book sized pages. They can really make the interior of your book look beautiful, and you will need this formatted file to upload to Amazon's KDP platform so your books can be published. Once you get the formatted manuscript back, you should have the epub, mobi, and PDF files that you need. Amazon makes it really easy to follow the steps uploading the proper files.

7. Speaking of reviews, I find it imperative that I make it as easy as possible early on for ARC readers to leave reviews. Once you get your book back from beta readers and tighten up your manuscript before sending it off to an editor, don't just sit idle while it's being edited. Get an ARC (advanced reader copy) group ready to rock so you can send it to them as soon as it's ready. You will have the formatted files to send these readers and they can upload it right to their kindle. The thing is, these advanced readers need a place to leave an early review, otherwise they may forget to come back on release day and leave one when Amazon allows. I highly recommend setting up the Goodreads page for the book early on in the process and would consider doing a cover reveal beforehand so you can add the cover image to the Goodreads page. That way, when ARC readers leave their early reviews, that cover image will start popping up in the world and sear itself into our horror-loving brains. Don't be afraid to give out a boatload of digital ARCs, because not everyone who takes it will leave a review. It's an unfortunate reality, but if I send out 50 copies, I'm happy to get 30 reviews out of it. The more advance reviews, the better. And the silver lining of it all? You will gain some avid followers in the process who feel they were part of your journey. They will become your core fan base and biggest supporters.

8. As important as ARC readers are, you will probably want to get your book to as many indie review sites, booktok, bookstagram reviewers as possible as well, because they can help spread the word quick. Not all of them will take books for review, but it's always worth sending as many of these influencers your book as possible. I'd research these people and network with them well before this step, though.

9. Give your release date plenty of time to breathe while you complete all these steps. So many indie authors get antsy and release their book as soon as it's formatted. While that works for some, I try to take a more patient approach and give myself around three months to promote, get reviews in, build the buzz, etc. As amazing as it is to get your book out into the world, it's even more amazing when people already recognize what it is on release day, and you can see a spike in sales right out of the gate.

10. When the book is out in the world, keep your foot on the gas and don't let up. Find ways to keep the book relevant when you hit those inevitable dips in sales. Keep people talking about the book. Whether you run contests, share reviews, run deals, or even give some books away, it all can help keep the book holding some sort of momentum well past release. Be sure to thank all involved on a regular basis. It really goes a long way. I'm talking about everything from editors/cover artist/formatter to your readers/reviewers/curators at bookstores. They are all part of your success, and they deserve to know that.

Before I go, I wanted to share a fun little story. I attended AuthorCon I as a fan, bringing physical ARCs of my book to hand out to my favorite authors in hopes they would read it. This was April 2022 and the book was released in June of that year. One of those authors I ran into was one of my all-time favorites in Ronald Malfi. He not only took a copy of my book, but asked me to sign it for him. I had talked with him on my podcast previously, so I wasn't completely new to him, but I was still nervous as hell about meeting one of my literary idols. As I started signing the book, he stops me mid signature and asks, "What the hell are you doing? Who taught you to sign a book that way?"

Confused, I asked what he meant. Well, I just so happened to be signing the inside cover, which is a big no-no. The worst part about it was that his copy was the last one I had to give out, and I had signed all of them that SAME way for the other authors. The rest of them had been too nice to call me out on it, but we had a good laugh about it, and I learned my lesson. Always sign the inside title page, not the inside cover. When AuthorCon II rolled around this year, I was lucky enough to have a table and actually sell books. Malfi had something to say about my second book as well, and I'll share it here. "A taut, nerve-jangling novel that puts Durgin's skills as an author on full display. Highly recommended."- Ronald Malfi, bestselling author of *Come With Me.*

    A lot can happen in the span of a year, people. Don't wait. Get to work and write that story. Chase those dreams, or should I say, "chase those nightmares."

Welcome to the Community
By
Natasha Sinclair

Independent horror is horror content and media created and published outside a traditional publishing house. Therefore, small press and self-published works come under the Indie Horror banner. Of course, you'll get all manner of 'what it means to me' sentiments from folks within the industry, but ultimately that's it.

***

It's deathly quiet outside the battered old oak door, except for an eerie low murmuring. It could be the wind from an ajar window keeping the cream-netted curtain in continuous motion. The window is stuck, it won't open further, nor will it close. An occasional shriek from the other side causes a jump — your heart has lodged itself in your throat, and every sphincter tightens. Anticipation crawls up your spine. *What if someone or something sees you?*

You reach for the brass knob; it's cold as ice and burns your sweaty palm. You pull back, hissing through your teeth and stifle the yelp from escaping your throat. Breathe. You close your eyes and open the door; just a crack, and tentatively peer in.

A buzzing infestation swarms every nook. A macabre rainbow of ghouls, ghosts and ghastly beasts buzz, honk, shriek, and squeal! No wonder it's so dark in here; there are bodies everywhere! From the rolling menacing mass, a creature parts itself and ambles towards you. This horror's head bends a little to its left as a regular-looking tortoiseshell cat is casually perched on its shoulder, purring. Your eyes widen. You've been seen, and there's nowhere to run! Even the cat doesn't calm the terror coursing through your muscles. You freeze. The dark-shrouded demonic menace reaches towards the door with its long boney, callused fingers and opens it wider. The wood groans, revealing you to the room of maniacs.

"Awright, man," it croaks in a garbled Scottish accent. "What's yer name?" It demands. You murmur your name, voice cracking. It nods, and a terrifying grin crawls up its long pale face. *Jeez. He looks like the crypt keeper,* you think. "A'm Kev," it grumbles cheerfully. The gaunt, egg-shaped-cunt's neck cracks as it turns 180 degrees to face the others, "Let's welcome the newbie to the community!"

***

The term community is often uttered among horror fans, readers and professionals alike. Evidence, perhaps, that even at a great distance, we're all seeking connection. Yes, even the darkest, most solitary parts of our hearts long for camaraderie, even if only occasionally. As wildly bizarre as that may seem to folk who negatively judge the genre and its participants from the outside. In truth, those that make up this community, whether they like that term or not, are among the most diverse groups of people from all corners of the globe with differing sexes, genders, race, languages, cultural, political, religious, spiritual, and economic backgrounds. Many are brought together with a passion for creative freedom and the desire to feel (or elicit) reactions and emotions that takes us away from our everyday realities. The provocative nature of horror and lack of constraints in indie horror fiction is perhaps a driving force behind the love, thirst, and feverish support for more!

My appreciation of indie horror stretches back to childhood. Watching forbidden hammer horror, comedic, religious, psychological, folk and, well, everything in the beautiful beast of a genre with my gran in her wee east-end Glasgow flat. Though it began with movies (at least in the fictional sense of horror), books sharply followed and took over my immersion in the genre. Perhaps my exposure in youth is the root of my anti-censorship stance and why this diverse, boundary-breaking genre has always serenaded me. I am horror's willing lover, and she can do anything she wishes with my insatiable mind. My position of that beginning as a consumer of horror has evolved over the years. I actively work in the field as a freelance professional editor under my brand 'Word Refinery', writer and independent publisher under 'Clan Witch' and 'Brazen Folk Horror', the latter with my literary partner Ruthann Jagge where we create our brand of fiercely female-led provocative independent horror that bends and blends genres.

Like any industry, many folks may enter the world performing in one area, but skill development is essential for personal and professional growth. If you're not striving to learn more, are you even living? The more intimate you can become with your craft, the better for you as a professional, for your peers and readers. This does not mean, however, that we can effectively turn our hands between skill sets because we hold mastery over one. This is perhaps the most common ignorance (or arrogance) that I've experienced and witnessed within the independent horror industry. Though, it applies as much to other genres. Because someone is a skilled guitarist, this doesn't automatically mean they can be as competent with any other instrument should they turn their attention. It's the same in writing, editing and publishing. Some skills can cross over but not entirely (not even close). And each of those three areas has a unique set of expertise, processes, and goals. Forming authentic connections that you can trust is vital.

While the openness, hospitality and even charity of the independent horror community is a fundamental draw, with it, there is a lot of tripe to wade through in terms of advice, quality, experience, expertise etc. Within the bustling masses, there are some outstanding individuals where quality matters, and where your voice (writers) matters, your expertise (editors, publishers) matters, your artistic skills (cover artists, designers, illustrators) matter. Folks who work hard and strive to eradicate the negative stigma associated with the indie horror business, and want to push hard to make their art better, or support writers through a skilful design, editorial and publishing relationships to make their story stand proud, more robust than it was when it landed on the editor's desk, wrapped in art that compliments the story, and reach readers through a reliable publisher. They're not always the loudest – the work comes first. In fact, those that know their stuff are usually the humbler and, above all, honest. If you ever see a self-professed grammar nazi sharing pages of errors they've found – know that a professional worth their salt would never be caught dead with such a label on their toe or shame a writer (editor or publisher's) work in such an immature, unprofessional, disrespectful fashion. Now someone who has a warped and misguided superiority complex that demands to be fed, maybe that's more the type. Ego makes the most mess, and many of us can regale tales of false promises or terrible advice from egomaniacs — reviewers, other writers, artists, editors or publishers that would send anyone considering opening the door running in search of an agent and a traditional route. Sometimes we can wrongly assign professional credibility due to their associations, time in the industry or output volume. Many aspects of creative industries are subjective, but not everything. There are clear-cut wrongs, too, of course.

Not every opportunity from a publisher or offer from someone who calls themselves an editor is in your best interest. As I always say, time is money. But it's more than that. Life is indeed short, and time invested is taken from something else. Doing something for the love of the genre, the books, or the community is one thing, but unless someone is being appropriately compensated for the time a project costs, what are they getting from it? Or are they doing that project justice if they are not spending the time it requires to make it the best it can be for you and your readers?

As a freelance editor, my time invested into a project and fees are aligned with my skill set, education and professional experience because I value my work and my clients. No one should work for free. Our time is not free; it's finite. With a few exceptions over the years — we've all done favours or exchanged professional services and skills — expect to pay for quality work if you have value in yours and respect your readers.

Among the rat traps and gormless ghouls behind that big door, there are some of the most beautiful and skilled souls in the world. I promise. And finding your tribe and those real connections to share ideas with and lift each other through friendships and professional relationships are invaluable to your experience in indie horror — as a fan or professional. The support and connections to the art can run deeper than family — visceral, no-holes-barred passion. Indie horror can be addictive. So, come on in. Get amongst it, don't be afraid and ride the waves that get your blood pumping. There's no judgment here. We love to try every flavour! Show us your demons. Who knows, it could be the making of you.

Now, close the door before the cat gets out. Kev won't be happy.

Don't do me any Favors

By

Mark Allan Gunnells

My name is Mark Allan Gunnells. Not a household name in the publishing industry, but I have been publishing in the small press for almost fifteen years now. I have released quite a few books (novels, novellas, short story collections), and worked with some wonderful publishers. I think that has earned me the right to give a little advice. What I want to focus on here is an important aspect to look for when deciding to go with a publisher.

Small press publishers don't really have the same kind of capital as the major New York Publishers, but they make up for that with passion and determination. There is also a certain freedom in the small press. New York publishing is too often all about marketing trends, wanting things that feel like things that are already successful. They can sometimes want to put their writers in a box and have them continually writing the same kind of story over and over because it has proven to sell. Small press allows writers to experiment and branch out, try new things, explore stories that are weird and unlike anything on the market. I have also noticed that particularly in the horror field, small press publishing is also much more open to queer voices which of course means a lot to me.

But, and surely you knew there was a but coming, not all small press publishers are created equal. There are publishers who promote more than others, some who do better covers, who offer a more diverse roster, etc. You will have to find the publishers that most suit your needs based on what you want to accomplish. However, no matter what you want to accomplish, allow me to give a bit of advice I think is applicable to every writer out there seeking a publisher.

If you encounter a publisher who acts like they are doing you a favor by publishing your work, turn around and run the other way.

Here's the thing about publishing, it is and should be a symbiotic relationship. Yes, you as the writer are getting something from the publisher (a home for your work, money, the chance to work with editors and cover artists), but the publisher is also getting something from you. Without your work there would be nothing for them to publish and they would make no money without authors providing them with content. Good publishers recognize that publishing isn't a one way street, and they treat their writers with the respect that entails.

There are publishers out there who do not understand this, who treat their authors as if publishing them is a favor and the writers should simply be grateful to be published and not expect anything more. These kinds of publishers rarely do any promotion, dumping your book onto the market with little to no fanfare. I've known publishers that barely even post about a release on social media, leaving all the promotion to the author. Now, working in the small press, a writer can expect to do a lot of self-promotion because small presses don't have the kind of marketing budget as a New York publisher. However, the good small press publishers understand that an author's reach only extends so far, and after a while can become shouting into an echo chamber. These publishers do their share of posting and sharing, foster relationships with podcasts and websites to help their writers find places to do interviews and post articles. They work with you trying to get the word out.

I've also found that publishers who feel they are doing you a favor by publishing you can be unreliable when it comes to many basic things you should expect from a publisher. Like answering emails in a timely manner, keeping you informed about sales, paying your royalties on time. When they feel they are being generous merely by publishing your work, these other things can come to feel less urgent to them. Also, they may not be as concerned with the editing process and cover art, because their attitude connotes a lack of professionalism that can result in a product of lesser quality.

To be perfectly frank, if you end up with this kind of publisher then it would actually have been better to simply self-publish your work because the publisher won't be providing you with any of the benefits of having an outsider publisher.

The good news is that I think these kinds of publishers are represented in smaller numbers than the publishers that do respect their authors. Publishers that understand publishing isn't an act of charity but a mutually beneficial arrangement work harder, are communicative, update you regularly on sales history and make payments on time. They use the best editors and cover artists they can get, they promote with you and don't expect you to do all the heavy lifting yourself. They treat every author on their roster as a success. They understand they aren't just giving you a gift by publishing, but you are doing something for them and they are doing something for you. It results in a relationship that increases the chances of success.

And the difference between these two kinds of publishers often has nothing to do with how prominent the publisher is. I have known of publishers with a lot of visibility who work with some pretty big names who treat the authors who aren't the "big names" like they did them a favor and put in no effort with their books, while upstarts that just came on the market hustle their asses off for their authors. Don't be blinded by prestige, look at how the publisher actually treats its writers. You want to go with the ones that treat ALL their writers as if they are "big names."

Publishing in the small press will always have its ups and downs, but I think you will be more primed for success when you avoid the publishers who treat you as charity. It really is the best favor you can do for yourself as an author.

Some Tips for the new (Indie Horror) Author
By
Kenzie Jennings

Based on my measly five years in this industry, here's my list of tips for the new (indie horror) author. Take what you need, trash what you don't:

1. Social Media is your friend...and your enemy. Tread carefully.

How can you possibly have a creative life in the 21st century if you don't have some sort of social media presence? For authors, it establishes a connection to others in the same community. I owe another creative, someone I've known since I was a toddler, for my introduction to social media, and he always managed to get me to sign on whatever platform was the next big thing. I owe yet another creative, Jeff Strand, whom I initially met on social media, my horror writing career.

I don't think I need to tell you how social media is the cheapest form of marketing for your work since that goes without saying. Another plus though: You'll meet other authors, editors, cover designers, publishers, and *readers* from all over the world. What could possibly be so wrong about that?

Well, we all know perfectly well that social media has its problems. It's not social media itself that's the issue when it comes to those creative connections. When terrible people obviously use it as a tool to do terrible things, it's problematic. Be careful how you interact with others. Be professional too. You're working after all. If you use social media as a free for all for yourself, hell, it's your profile. You may certainly do what you want, say what you want, project yourself as whatever you want. *However*, remember, someone, somewhere, is taking screenshots of some of the awful shit you may be posting and/or reposting. Your social media profiles should represent the best of you, not the worst of you. Keep that other stuff private, you psychopath.

2. If someone you respect in the industry offers you advice, it doesn't hurt to take it.

Pay attention to them, learn from them, *listen* to them. If I had closed myself off to advice, I would've never gone to KillerCon and met my publisher, which would've made my publishing journey probably a lot longer.

3. Speaking of KillerCon, if you have the time and extra money, invest in a trip to a writers' convention or conference.

A convention (or conference) is your chance to meet others and talk to them one-on-one. I hate using the word "networking" because it sounds so cold and corporate. A writers' conference is generally warm and inviting, and a good one will inspire and invigorate you. The smaller the convention, obviously, the more likely you'll get to actually hang out with people you admire. If you're an introvert like I am, it will seem daunting, and the butterflies never really go away. That being said, plenty of authors are introverts, too, and feel the exact same way. You know this though. We're in a lonely profession where, sometimes, the only company around is living in our heads. I have this problem where I tend to make an ass of myself in front of people I admire, but now that I've seen them interacting with others, I've also discovered that they have their own quirks and insecurities as well.

I won't sugarcoat it though. There will be moments when you'll meet someone whose work you admire, and that person will disappoint you when you meet them. (It's happened to me a few times now.)

However, for every author who's snubbed you, there are several more who are as interested in you as you are with them. Stick with them. Your world will become richer with them in it.

4. Envy is a bitch. Stay away from bitches.

Avoid comparing yourself to someone else. Don't let thoughts about them consume you. It's not easy, I know. In fact, as I'm sitting here, reworking this, it's struck me that over the past several months, I've been struggling internally with my own envy of several other splatterpunk/extreme horror authors. I just have to consistently remind myself that their success has *nothing to do* with my success. Envy is one of the greatest flaws of the human condition, but if you let it take control, it will cut a hole in you and fill it with acid. It's hard to shake that sour, curdling feeling, but for me, the feeling somewhat subsides when I remind myself that their path is not *my* path...

There's a little mind trick I taught myself years ago back when I was an amateur performer. I always thought acting was a lot of fun. How often is it you get to pretend to be someone else in front of an audience and not get arrested for identity theft? Anyway, during my early years living in central

Florida, I was involved in a local improv group and a little community theater. It was a great way to creatively cut loose and meet some wonderful people who enjoyed the same thing I did. At some point though, it grew difficult for me, and envy seemed to be the culprit.

It dawned on me that I'd been handling envy the wrong way when a good friend of mine, whom I met at an audition, said to me that when we'd first met, she'd been aiming for the part that I wound up getting. However, the director had seen something different in her, so he gave her a key role that turned out to be perfect for her—a role, I might add, that was wonderfully memorable because of what she'd brought to the character. That's when I realized that what had been right for me hadn't been right for her… and what had been right for her hadn't been right for me.

Subsequently, *that* became how I approach envy. Envy only enters the picture when we compare ourselves to others who are not like us, and when we want what they have, it often makes little sense because what they have isn't necessarily what is right for us in the moment.

So when it comes to envy of other authors' successes, ask yourself if what they have is what's right for you, too. More than likely...

> A) it may not be your time just yet
> B) they may be writing about something that just isn't your thing
> C) they may have caught onto a particular trend that publishers are looking for in the moment
> D) they might be working with a publisher

(and/or agent) who isn't right for *you*

If you are persistent and hardworking at your craft, your time will come. Just don't let someone else's success determine your own.

5. Watch how you handle negative reviews.

I reminded my fiction writing class this term that **their writing isn't for everyone**, and that's perfectly fine. Same goes for you. You know yourself, and you know your audience. That's what matters.

Every author I've interacted with seems to have different ways in how they handle negative reviews. Some read them for critical content they think may help them. Some vent about them to their friends and family. Some turn them into comedy (Inspired by others, I'm seriously thinking about turning some of mine into bookmarks). And so on.

One piece of crucial advice they share in common though is that you should *never* directly respond to negative reviews and to the reviewers who write them.

For the most part, reviewers aren't writing for you. They're writing for other *readers*. When you insert yourself into it, you're going to alienate reviewers and the readers they're writing for. They're not going to want to read anything of yours again. That may sound ideal to you, but from what I've learned, writing communities are pretty small. The indie horror writing community in particular is smaller than one might think. Sooner or later, word will get around that you got ugly with a reviewer on social media, on Goodreads, in an online group…somewhere, anyway… and watch your reputation go down the toilet.

So do not engage.

6. You're only as good as your next project.

You will ALWAYS be asked what you're working on next, so you should be working on something new, moving forward not backwards. I find it hard to keep from worrying about the state of my published work and its potential readership. I confess I also spend too much time honing in on a previous project and lose track of what I *ought* to be concentrating on. So I have to keep reminding myself that my debut novel, *Reception*, was a project that kept me from solely focusing on what was happening to my previous novel that was *supposed* to be my debut, a novel that is now in limbo, and I really don't mind that it is because I've moved forward. In other words, current projects are the healthier distractions.

Again, forward not backwards.

7. No one wants to hear about your book...unless they've *asked you about your book*.

Now I know, for the most part, we're in charge of pitching and our advertising for our new book. That being said, the only person who's totally invested in your book is you until you've a reader base, and for most authors, that doesn't happen overnight. Even if you've readers for your work though, the book isn't as important as you are as a human being.

Connect with people as people do. Stop making it all about your work. No one gives a shit about it until they do…on their own time…out of their own interest for it.

Again, I'm not trying to say don't advertise your work, but I've seen authors who've done nothing but plug their work over and over and over again and do nothing else. And you know what? It's not a good look.

8. You are never too young or too old to start a writing career.

I started this journey as a published horror writer at 46. I'll be frank; it's been a continuous struggle for me to feel at ease in the horror community as a middle-aged woman. It's totally an internal thing caused by no one but my own insecurities. I'm getting there though. Everyone—and I mean everyone—has been gracious and kind, warm and welcoming. I've had an iffy moment or two with a couple of authors (see #3), but they weren't the norm whatsoever. So if I can jumpstart a career like this in my late 40s, think about what YOU can do.

9. Know your limits. Say "yes" only to the opportunities that you know you'll be able to do.

I'm in awe of authors who tackle multiple projects. I've had to accept the fact that I can't though, especially during a busy semester (I teach freshman comp. at a community college). By the end of the semester, I'm so mentally exhausted, I need a week where I don't read or write much just to decompress. Then instead of plunging straight into a big project, I start small. It works for me. Do whatever works for you.

However, don't ever assume you're obligated to do everything that comes your way. Oh, you'll definitely be tempted because you'll have that persistent, nagging voice in the back of your mind warning you your career is over if you pass on opportunities and invites. Bullshit. If you can't, you can't, and that's okay. Remember, don't compare yourself to your peers. Know. Your. Limits.

10. Adapt or die.

Your job as a writer who wants a readership is to write for those readers. Yeah, okay, you're writing for yourself, you're writing what YOU want to read… yadda yadda…but let's be real. You want readers. That's why you're in this business. But here's the thing…you'd better be cognizant of what is acceptable and what isn't in the 21st century. We are not living in a *Mad Men* universe where things like racism, homophobia, and misogyny are (insidious) sociocultural norms. If you can't stand the thought of contemporary norms infringing on your right to be a shitstain, and you want to flaunt your defiance, be prepared to watch your career die.

During my short time in the horror community, I've already seen several people in the community self-destruct their careers due to their dirtbag behavior. I don't know why they thought they were going to get away with any of it since this is also the age of screenshots (see #1). A part of me thinks they wanted to be caught, like it was some kind of weird, masochistic pull or something…or that infamy was the way to go (controversy brings the sales, sure, but your reputation is officially in the gutter).

You have to be a better human than that. Adapt to the modern world, or watch your career go down in flames.

11. Always be gracious, and credit everyone involved.

Unless you really did *everything* yourself, your book, your baby, is an overall community creation. You did the bulk of the work in writing it, and it's *your* original story/premise, but if you're working with a traditional publisher—OR you're commissioning editors, cover artists, formatters, etc., as a self-publisher—you've a team that's working with you to make the book into something truly special. Thank all of them, and acknowledge them. Even better, point others in their direction, helping them with their business, too.

That's all I wanted to share with you, my fellow indie horror authors, for now anyway. Until then, keep at it...

Always keep at it.

Choosing a Publisher
By
Chad Lutzke

Being a writer is definitely one career where you can actually benefit from your mistakes made. Each one teaches you a valuable lesson on what to do next time and who to stay away from. Searching for a publisher you can trust is one of those lessons every author needs to learn. My hope is you can avoid a pitfall or two by paying attention to what I've learned.

I'm what is called a "hybrid" author. Many of my books are independently published, meaning I release them myself, and others are through small presses. I'm obviously aware of my own capabilities, but when it comes to other publishers handling my books I need to put them under the microscope before signing any offered contract.

After that contract is signed, everything turns to hindsight. Initially, things may look just fine. But months down the road, you may realize your publisher isn't as adequate as you'd thought. You're not getting paid on time. They're doing nothing to promote you. They're alienating half your potential audience by ranting on Twitter. They may be nice people, but not every nice person with a passion for books is business saavy.

I've been with publishers who didn't pay their authors, ones who never promoted, ones who politically ranted on social media on the regular, and ones you don't realize were born to fail until you get a peek behind the curtain.

Handing over a manuscript you've toiled over the last several months/years is no delicate matter. So, below are six bits of advice to help you choose a publisher worth getting into bed with.

1. Ask around. Once, when signing up with a problem publisher, I did ask around. The problem is I only asked one person, and that person happened to be the publisher's "golden egg." Golden eggs are going to be treated differently. They're going to be given special attention and paid on time. What I should have done is ask lesser-known authors how they're being treated, if they're getting paid, and if they're happy with the attention they've gotten as well as effort toward promo. Don't ask the golden egg. They'll most likely not be privy to what's really going on.

2. Visit the publishers website. Make sure it's up to date. If the last three books they put out aren't even listed, there's some laziness afoot, and it's a red flag. They're not doing their job.

3. Visit their social media pages. If your publisher uses the same place to promote your hard work as they do to promote their political opinions—even if you agree with those opinions—just know they are alienating an audience. Social media is the worst place for political discussion anyway. Because there is no discussion. It's bitching, looking for like-minded bitchers. Whether you're bitching about how slow service was at the restaurant last night or how much you hate the president or someone else's views, this causes negative somatic markers, which are like little parasites the reader soaks in, letting them know, even on a subconscious level, this place is not a good time. That's why everyone likes hanging out with the person who makes them feel good. Sure, most of us love dark movies and dark books. But when it comes to living life, we all just want to be happy and to maintain that happiness. By constantly bitching, you're poisoning yourself, and if that publisher can't treat their own company with respect and professionalism, they're losing sales and driving people away, and this hurts you.

4. Take note of book sales. Look at the roster of books the publisher has to offer. Check the

sales rankings and reviews on Goodreads and Amazon. Do take note that at least the first 10-20 reviews on a book are usually friends or acquaintances of the author who are going to offer kind words no matter what. Read recent reviews. The ones from complete strangers who have no obligation to stroke the author. If the reviews state things like "Loaded with errors...needed to be edited" that's a red flag. The publisher may not be doing their job.

    5.   The book covers. Are they good? A lot of authors and publishers are using AI art these days so the art may be good but the font and placement godawful. Pay attention to that. Also, have you been seeing the book cover all over Twitter and Instagram? If so, that's a good sign the publisher is doing their job promoting.

    6.   Ask to see a contract. Look it over carefully. If you're not familiar with current rates, ask around. And make sure the publisher isn't asking for movie rights. I probably don't need to expand on this. Also, make sure you're getting copies of your own book. I'm not talking e-copies. Get those trophies for the shelf. You shouldn't have to pay for a copy of your own book. If a publisher like Thunderstorm Books can offer their authors two to three copies of a limited hardcover that goes for

$100 a piece, a publisher can definitely offer you a few paperbacks.

Diary of A Dreamer
By
Jim Ody

Introduction:

My name is Jim and this is my story.

I've always loved horror. There is something damn right honest about it. The world in which we live is far from teddy bears, fluffy clouds and gentle kisses and more about heartache, anxiety, pain and hatred. Too many times we try to shield the young from reality, instead happy to paint the world with sugar-coated Disney lies, then wonder why when reality bites they upgrade Haribo sweets and sports clubs for prescription drugs and therapy.

As a youngster, I enjoyed being scared. From my obsession with the Scooby-Doo gang into the foray of adult horror movies and books, I knew I had an interest in the macabre. I've always maintained a good moral compass, but I was intrigued by all that surrounded the unknown.

My sister is three years my elder and exposed me to horror movies at an early age. I remember being scared of the Michael Caine movie *The Hand*, and also *An American Werewolf in London,* but soon I was watching *The Omen*, and *Amityville Horror* before being obsessed with the Friday the 13th franchise (which I still am today).

I flirted with journalism before I realised I was pretty much a ghostwriter. A faceless robot tapping out reviews of rock bands that their management wanted the world to read. My integrity was compromised and I would no longer allow the puppeteers to control me.

My peers were never interested in writing. Most didn't understand the fascination with books, either. I remember a time at college, caught with my nose in a paperback and being made to feel like I had been discovered with a pornographic magazine of dark and specialist taste.

"Your sort don't read books," he stated. Well, that's where you're wrong. You see, I've always indulged in things that made me feel good. I was the class clown, first and foremost, but also enjoyed sports. I played the drums and always had headphones on, listening to something antisocial. The popular lads didn't understand me. I'd happily high-five them, skip classes to play football and frequent the odd parties, but I was never part of their circle. I was drawn to the stoners (though never one myself); the ones that looked like losers from the outside but whom I found to be more genuine. They didn't care about what people thought and lived their lives for the moment ☐ plus I preferred the hippy-girls who hung around them, who talked about their favourite serial killers rather than which pop idol they had a crush on. To this day, the smell of incense conjures up visions of bedrooms adorned with zodiac designs, crystals, and flashes of pierced nipples. It was a time of expression.

What is horror?

This, dear reader, is a good time to talk about genres. When I first started to write, I did so as a horror author, but in the '90s there was a change. As a hangover from the drug-fueled party highs, the debauched misogynists flaunting the sexualization of women, and, of course the great Satanic Panic pandemic, censorship appeared like some zombie from a grave and with it followed hordes of lawyers, government officials and parents wielding invisible torches of fire and pitch-folks resulting in horror being shunned and sent packing from the mainstream.

This brings us to the spiders analogy. Rock band Motley Crue's bassist, leader, and overdose-survivor, Nikki Sixx once said the reason why people's first instinct was to kill any arachnid was our lack of understanding. People have an inherent need to kill what they don't understand. He was talking about rock, but this also applies to horror. We live in a world where it's easy to spout good and evil like everything is simply black and white; however you only need to watch the daily news for ten minutes to know that evil has a mundane normality far scarier than fiction. It doesn't wear a mask with horns, parade around in a bloodstained jumpsuit, nor have sharp fangs, but, in fact, resembles you and I. Evil is hidden in plain sight and that is a notion that as horror writers we can play on. It's more shocking. We drop our defenses and often trust those we should be running from. Many a great twist has used this trope.

To get around this shunning, the literary industry looked more closely at their author's book plots, and anything that involved a human killer could now be deemed crime, then quickly the supernatural, and monster books slipped into backrooms and under the counter like some pornographic contraband of the dead, whilst the rebranded books gained a huge following, large advances, big promotion and made authors of the genre household names. They killed horror because they didn't understand it; they didn't recognise the draw it had.

This was in a time before Amazon's monopoly on the world, and even before the internet was anything more than a digital desire for the rich. I was left searching for publishers in a large paperback book packed with details of companies quick to state they would not entertain horror. Publishers didn't want the new Stephen King, as he wasn't yet pushing up daisies and remained prolific. They also deemed him a one-off. Despite all this, I was a huge Richard Laymon fan and also scooped up books from the likes of Dean Koontz, Bentley Little, Jack Ketchum and Scott Nicholson.

The film industry was a little more forgiving. An unspoken deal had been made with a secret Hollywood handshake, and Kevin Williamson was able to resurrect the slasher trope by adding a new spin and reducing the nudity, but the literary business stayed strong and stoic in its continued suppression.

My Writing Journey:

Horror authors are the black sheep of the literary world. Our skin must grow thick as we dodge the verbal jabs and projectiles sent hurtling our way. We are the spiders crawling on floors minding our own business to whom others don't understand and feel the need to squash and eradicate from this planet.

I don't care. The hatred only fuels my passion further to write openly and freely, without consent. I refuse to be gagged or shackled to the laptop. I've done that.

Now I was an easy-influenced teenager, my shocking fashion sense testament to that, and I was brainwashed into turning my back on horror in favour of crime. I'm not proud of my decision, but I was also sporting a ponytail at the time, and distracted by gangsta rap. We all have our crosses to bear.

By the early '00s, I had written a couple of books. I'd had a fleeting interest from an agent which I probably read into more than was there, but the gatekeepers stood fast, and it was at this point I fell into music journalism. It was quick and easy, and within a week I had recognition from my unique style. For a few brief years, I was quoted multiple times in musical press releases and thanked in a few bands' album acknowledgments. Fast forward to 2010, and now a father of two, I was disillusioned by the journalism world. Even churning out the odd comedic articles became mundane. I was entertaining a very small crowd. I concentrated on writing my next book and entered it into the Amazon Scout program, now defunct, where you get votes for your book and Amazon uses this as a way to see who will make them money, and they would offer them a contract. Another genius entrepreneurial move by them. I've never been top of the podium when it came to popularity contests. At best I'm described as 'odd' (an English teacher told my parents I had good stamina – more of a nod towards ADHD), but what it did do was prove that people outside my DNA were there supporting my book. Undeterred, I self-published it. For the next few years, I wrestled with a few publishers and was burned more times than I care to admit (I still have a publisher with four of my novels and three of my audiobooks who hasn't sent me royalties in three years), but what is it they say? What doesn't kill you makes you stronger? Or some such crap.

Writing is about the enjoyment of the craft. You cannot be swayed into fitting yourself into a box that's not designed for you. Being a literary contortionist is not the right way to go. Nor is being a people pleaser. You cannot ever satisfy everybody, so why try?

Themes and Settings:

My childhood helped to develop how I write my themes and the settings I use.

I grew up on a farm in the middle of nowhere. Literally. It made trick-or-treating challenging and something only the kids in town did. My nearest neighbours were so far away I assumed at one point one might be *The Waltons* whilst the others the Ingles from *Little House on The Prairie* (some of you may need to Google these); alas, they were neither. So large towns and cities were not settings I could relate to. The big smoke was not the backdrop I thought about for escapism, and I could never be scared when surrounded by others; there was always a child crying, random laughing, hysterical women, traffic, horns blasting, dogs barker and the general cacophony of city life – although at night people lock themselves away, or take to the shadows, but after dark in the city was where I stayed away from (I'd experienced some scary times in LA, so that was enough for me!).

For me, fear is isolation. Surrounded by your own thoughts and a threat that can be anything from human to supernatural to some kind of beast. Growing up in the middle of nowhere nurtured this sentiment.

However, I am very character driven. I like to look at my cast and explain why they do the things they do. We all have unique traits that we may've been born with, or life has molded our psyche into acting the way we do. But to be the sole player allows the hero to be clever and chose their options wisely, and that's why there always needs to be at least another person. Someone the protagonist cares for and who clouds their judgement. It's like the *Dungeons &*

Dragons cartoon, which used to annoy me. They'd almost get home every episode, but someone would be left so they'd have to stay. The emotional ties are hugely important.

In terms of settings, I favour woods, lakes, and coastal towns and like to weave in a slice of supernatural that's not the main plot driver but a tease to make you question reality. I want my readers to feel something. I want them to question what they'd do and how they'd feel – but mostly I wish for them to be entertained. The lines between fact and fiction should blur. Most of my plots you cannot say could not happen, and that's the seed I like to plant.

When I think about my books, there is often a sense of loss. It might be a missing person, a broken relationship, or even the protagonist searching for themselves after poor life decisions. I think these are all subtle horrors that frame the story to help with the main unease of the plot. Often, the creature is not the worst thing in the book; it's the situation that we've created for ourselves.

Conclusion:

Horror has carved its niche and built a huge underground following of readers and indie authors who have spilled into mainstream. There is still a huge stigma attached to the genre. I recently sold my books at a local craft market and had people look at my banner, then at me like I was some sort of sex pest. People visibly walked around my table and audibly muttered, "Not for me!" like I might have some epiphany and write about romantic teenage vampires instead.

What is becoming more evident is the acceptance of books that flirt with horror. We're resigned to seeing our books appear in groups of psychological/thrillers, mystery, and crime genres where the members would never entertain that these books are deeply rooted in horror, but do you know what? That's fine.

The horror community is like no other. The readers and authors are hugely supportive, and there is a desire to own the paperback versions of books over ebooks, which is unique and something that should be applauded.

Horror is here to stay, with more and more books going viral and making it to either the big screen or snapped up by the likes of Netflix, Amazon Prime and other subscription channels.

There is still so much to explore in this world that is strange, weird and downright horrific.

The world is a dark place, and it's one I wish to explore further.

Change the Music, Keep the Melody
By
Brennan LaFaro

Being a writer brings with it an unspoken pressure to showcase originality and uniqueness, to be a veritable unicorn among horses. If you want the bookstores to make space on their shelves for your tiny tome, you'd better have created something that "defies comparison". But this is largely bullshit. A walk through the rows at your local store shows mafia books that offer modern retellings of the Godfather, romance books featuring the same bodice-ripping covers on display thirty, forty years ago, and "literary fiction" that is just a spin on Huckleberry Finn setting out for the territories.

To be clear, giving new life and modern sensibilities to classic stories and tropes isn't wrong. It's a conversation, and often, it's one we're not even aware of having until after the fact. As writers, we're readers first and once we join the ranks of the gilded pen, it's easy to eschew every lesson, every peculiar idea, we've stowed away on some dusty shelf in the back of our brain.

In early 2020, I read a book that changed my life. It didn't make me sell my belongings and move to Mongolia or stop eating meat. All it did was alter the way I saw dialogue in books, and the way it can affect story and character. The thing is, even a miniscule shift in trajectory can send one careening off the beaten path. That book was *Cold in July* by Joe R. Lansdale, and in those 300 pages, I became a student, watching Mr. Lansdale make each one of those words mean something. Every piece of dialogue that some might label as throwaway gave insight into the characters the reader inhabited a cramped truck cabin with. I learned very quickly that whenever a character opens their mouth, the writer has an opportunity to plant a seed in the reader's mind that may not matter, may not even make sense for a hundred pages. Nevertheless, that seed has been planted.

Fast forward to later that year, and you'd find me knee deep in writing my second book following *Slattery Falls*. A novella-length story called *Last Stay* about an Arizona motel run by a murderous couple. The story intrigued me because I got to explore themes such as how a marriage survives under pressure and how far people will go to justify their actions. Neither of those themes were the spark that brought the story to life and made me think a reader might want to spend their time with it, however.

As a new-ish writer, I believed in pacing and action. I still do, of course, but in a way that's a little less black and white. That former binary brain told me something should happen at all times to keep the reader engaged. Bam! A murder. Pow! Cleaning up the body and oh shit, is that the police? Shazam! Car chase.

That's the type of story I set out to create, and somewhere along the way, I found myself with pages and pages of conversations. Between John Parker and his wife, Faye. Between John and Buck, a traveling salesman. Between the kids in a car, fresh out of college and crossing the country. My inclination was to cut, prune, and hack away at these chatty harbingers of boredom. Except they didn't bore me. They told me why I should care when someone questioned their goodness, why characters performed the actions they did. So, I left them as is. When you have trusted beta readers—"trusted" being the operative word—they'll let you know they fell asleep at page thirty, and could you please, for the love of all things, add a fistfight?

Instead, early feedback was that the plot could use a couple tweaks here and there, but the dialogue brought the story to life. So, I tweaked, and I hid the book away and eventually I found a home for it with D&T Publishing. Before sending it out for blurbs, I gave the manuscript a pass and that dark bulb floating above my head flickered. First an ember, then a whole fireworks show. *Last Stay* owed a gracious chunk of its personality to *Cold in July*. The stories have no clear parallels and if you skip the dedication—To Joe, of course—you'd never know. But I know now. I caught myself red-handed, nodding my head to another writer's work like I dug what the drummer was doing, and then performing the literary equivalent of, 'I like what you bring to the table, now it's my turn to solo'. Jazz musicians do this all the time. Whether it's because of harmonic structure or just listening to another instrument take center stage before it's your turn to blow, those influences trickle in and inform the music that's about to come out of you.

Another pristine example of this philosophy is *Noose*, my horror western. With this book, the conversation began with Death's Head Press. They just didn't know it. Like most of the indie horror world, their splatter westerns grabbed me by the shirt collar and demanded my attention. Engrossing stories by talented authors will do that, but just like *Cold in July*, I found myself asking books like Wile E. Young's *The Magpie Coffin* and Kenzie Jennings' *Red Station*, what truly makes this combination click? We like blood and gore, we're horror people, but what is it about the 1800s American west that lends itself so well to the multitude of stories and sub genres that can take place there?

The Magpie Coffin sat me down and slung an arm around my shoulder. It said, "Here there be monsters, and they don't have to hide in the shadows". The time and setting lends itself to lawlessness and a moral shade of gray any horror writer worth their salt would froth at the mouth to work with. Mike Ennenbach's *Hunger on the Chisholm Trail* nodded its head and said, "That's all true, but consider this". The unexplored frontier is the ocean depths, the solitude of space, of the 19th century. Nobody knew exactly what was out there waiting, nobody could be sure, and the job of the horror writer is to look into the unknown and dream up the worst it has to offer. No matter how improbable. And with each successive release, my mind took notes.

When the time came, I opened up a new document and wrote, "NOOSE, by Brennan LaFaro, a splatter western". About eight pages later, I deleted the last three words. It's the beauty of conversation, really. You're not beholden to blindly agree with everything the other person says. You can cherry pick the horrors hiding in the shadows, the characters so brash and awful, the idea of them roaming free comes complete with goosebumps, and any other glowing aspect of the dark frontier that tickles your fancy. It also leaves you free to say, but what if I focused more on the adventure aspect, the nature of the quest? Keep the horror in horror western, sprinkle in the supernatural, but ultimately find a way to change the key of the song without losing the melody, if we're going to keep music metaphors alive.

And for the record, *Noose* may not fit squarely in the splatter western box, but it's not afraid to throw the red stuff around.

So it goes, and it could go on for days. We could talk about how I discovered that *Slattery Falls* is a vampire book well over a year after its publication, and only then because of a reread of an all-time great, *Salem's Lot*. That particular conversation with Mr. King influenced the *Slattery* sequels more than a little. We could talk about the effect of listening to and responding to music throughout short stories and sometimes full-length novels. Dear reader, if we ever meet up in person, buy me a drink and I'll burden you with the lengthy list of artists and albums that make the heart of my writing beat.

Here it is. We're artists and we like art. We don't just like it because it's pretty, or it sounds nice. We like it because it claws its way into every pore and enters our bloodstream. It shoots through arteries and veins, finding its way to our brains where it lodges like an embolism. When something like that becomes a part of you, it's bound to seep into unexpected aspects of our lives.

When you're feeling like your work is trite and cliché, remember that there's not another soul in the world that can write a story in your voice. As a rule, readers aren't looking for you to reinvent the wheel, they're looking for you to engage them, and maybe the best way to do that is to give them something familiar to latch onto that's told in a new and exciting way. Change the music but keep the melody. Interviews and articles are phenomenal resources, but to truly learn how to tell stories, the best conversations are with the stories themselves. Hunter S. Thompson did not retype *The Great Gatsby* to improve his dexterity on a typewriter and Miles Davis did not play sets full of standards because he couldn't write his own tunes. They simply recognized that, in order to create art, one must embrace art.

Paint it Dark
~ Creating an eerie atmosphere and foreshadowing ominous events ~
By
Simon Clark

'Oooh, that's scary.' This could be your reaction if you're reading a well-written horror story. Yet what is *present* in the text that scares? Is it when the werewolf attacked, or the vampire pounced, or the monster roared? Probably not. I'm pretty sure those shivers started to trickle deliciously down your spine when you read the early parts of the story, when, for example, the character first sets eyes on the haunted house.

I write horror. My job is to frighten. But I aim to frighten in a way that is enticing and pleasurable. So many writers who are new to horror rush their character to a scene where there is full-blooded carnage that disgusts or shocks the reader. Gruesome excess soon becomes tedious.

If we're agreed that the best horror fiction requires some careful scene setting before the truly horrific action takes place, then I'd invite you to join me in the exercises that follow this introductory essay.

Before we reach the nitty-gritty of the exercises I'd like to tell you why they are important to my own writing. As I've already said, my job is to frighten. So when I'm writing a description of a house, or even the weather, I'm mindful that it should not be a plain description of architecture or of rain. I ask myself what trigger words I can employ that tell the reader that ghostly events are on their way, or that the hero is heading relentlessly toward danger.

The easiest way for me to demonstrate this is to present an example of the kind of fiction I write. What follows are the opening lines from my novel *Vengeance Child:* -

The midnight rain did not whisper. It struck the big house hard. Rain clattered at windows. Drops hit the patio table in a salvo of vicious bangs. Heaven's bullets. A sound like war. As if the earth had been invaded from above. Take no prisoners. Batter the house into the ground...

So, why did I write the first paragraph of my novel in such a way? By the time you've completed the exercises you will have found the answer. What's more, you'll be writing fiction that makes the reader shiver and murmur, 'Oooh, that's scary.'

EXERCISE

Generally, eerie fiction will contain certain words and phrases that serve as something akin to hypnotic suggestion. That is to say, they implant in the reader's mind the notion that uncanny events are approaching, and that characters will find themselves in danger from perhaps an inexplicable or supernatural source. The use of these key words and phrases might be termed 'the language of horror.'

'The Signal-Man' by Charles Dickens is well-worth studying. This deceptively simple ghost story opens with the narrator visiting a signal-man who is based in his signal-box beside a railway line. Right at the beginning of the tale the narrator gazes at the railway line, which emerges from a tunnel. Notice those powerful trigger words in the following: -

... the gloomier entrance to a black tunnel, in whose massive architecture there was a barbarous and forbidding air. So little sunlight ever found its way to this spot, that it had an earthy deadly smell, and so much cold wind rushed through it, that it struck chill to me, as if I had left the natural world.

A less talented author might have written 'The railway line emerged from the dark tunnel.' The genius of Dickens mesmerises the reader with his adroit use of words. He reinforces the fact it is dark with the use of 'gloomier' and 'black.' The phrase 'so little sunlight' drives the point home. He describes the architecture as 'barbarous', so he's imbuing the structure with an air of violence. Again, the threat is reinforced by the smell of the earth being 'deadly.' Dickens evokes the cold and the eerie gloom of the place then prepares us for the supernatural horror to come by announcing that the character feels as if he's 'left the natural world.'

Practice this technique with these short exercises (half a page is ample): -

1. Describe a haunted house. Firstly, talk about the house in plain terms. For example, 'The house was built from brick. Its windows looked out over the park.' Then insert trigger words to imbue the house with an uncanny aura. Perhaps like this: 'The old, dilapidated house was built from bricks that were the colour of blood. Its windows looked out over the park. They resembled cold, staring eyes as they regarded that forbidding and lonely realm of trees, which harboured the shadows of night.'

2. Describe a sinister stranger. Experiment with trigger-words that suggest something is dangerously amiss with our stranger. Pay attention to the eyes. For example, 'His eyes had a spectral glow.' Or: 'ghost-lights glinted in her eyes.' Or: 'In the stranger's eyes, she

glimpsed the suffering of a thousand orphaned children.' Be adventurous!

3. Using the language of horror, describe a stretch of river as it flows beneath a city bridge.

4. Convey the menace of a tree where witches were once hanged long ago. Are its branches like hooked fingers clawing at the sky? Does its 'brutal trunk' loom over the road? Do 'monstrous patterns in the bark' suggest evil faces? Does the shadow it cast 'chill the blood and darken the meadow'? And when the breeze passes through its leaves what sound does it make? Sighs? Whispered voices? Chuckling sounds? Can you describe the tree so it seems that you're describing a malicious and violent monster? Or can you describe that melancholy old tree in such a way the reader feels as if they are reading about the tragic victims who ended their lives there?

Of course, you can continue with these exercises of your own devising. You can vary them: describe a cat found locked in an abandoned church, or a truck owned by a psychopath, or a gold broach belonging to a woman who poisoned her first husband – and the second, and the third!

The object of these exercises is this: to use the power of words to transform the ordinary into the extraordinary. Weave words and phrases in such a way that the description of a tree, or a house, or even an ordinary-looking supermarket becomes the electrifying evocation of a frightening, haunted place.

Free Therapy
By
Mark Towse

You'll probably get more advice than you can handle in this little treasure trove of a book, so I'll instead focus on how writing changed my life. Now, I know that sounds corny as all hell, cheesier than a cheese ball, but I'm confident the following story will put pay to thoughts of it being anything other than the truth. And if it doesn't, ask my wife.

Until five years ago, I was getting through a bottle of red wine every night just to numb myself from mundanity. It got to a point where it hardly touched the sides. That's not a boast; I was in a bad way. Somehow, I was still surfing and running five miles a day, but no matter how hard I tried to leave the dark cloud behind, the demons within had me in their sights and were catching up quickly. Most of my time was spent behind a mask, nodding in the right places, performing husbandry and fatherhood to the best of my limited ability, but the veil was slipping. When it all became too much one day, I jumped in the car and took off for a drive with no destination in mind. Within five minutes, I had to pull over, tears streaming and my throat hoarse from screaming, a desperate attempt to rid myself of all the bile I'd bottled up for decades.

"You're always talking about it. Why don't you give it a shot?" Those were the words that left my amazing wife's lips when I finally returned home that day, mask-less and the last of my pride left out on the road. "I think I might," I replied.

So, at the ripe old age of forty-five years old, my writing journey began. And it was always going to be about the horror, ever since getting my first library card and picking up Cujo from the local library. Horror is limitless and the perfect arena to invite one's demons for battle. No more running.

Even then, I had no real idea what I was getting myself into and that I would shortly become hooked. "I'd sell my soul to the devil if it meant I could write full-time" is a quote from one of my earlier bios, and it still stands today. I should warn anyone thinking of beginning this journey or who has recently hopped on board that writing is dangerously addictive. No, I mean *dangerously.* I recommend setting up a mini-schedule and sticking it on the fridge. It's an inelegant but marriage-saving device that will let everyone know when you are unavailable. Who knows? You might even avoid getting hit in the head with a saveloy.

True story.

That said, since picking up that pen and losing myself in that first slice of *magic* world, the demons that haunted me have become nothing more than an occasional whisper. When writing, I'm untouchable, wholly immersed in the environment, all my excess energy and emotions bleeding onto the page. The rush I get when I'm 'in the flow' is hard to describe, but it feels oh-so-right. Time is different, as quick as the summer holidays from yesteryear. You blink, and as though emerging from a dream-like haze, you have three thousand words on the page and another adventure under your belt.

I fucking love it!

We live and breathe through our characters. We join them on their travels, whether in this world or the next. We are without bounds, untethered by the constraints of society, as free as a bird that can transcend universes. It's the perfect excuse to drop the mask and face our traumas, becoming as raw and vulnerable as we wish, without judgement and fear of repercussion.

In summary, writing horror is the best therapy in the world, and I recommend it to all. When I'm truly immersed, hanging on my characters' words, inhaling the smells of whatever environment I'm creating, an overwhelming sense of peacefulness washes over me to the point of feeling almost meditative. There's nothing like it. And when I start talking to my wife about it, she also glazes over... but I think that's because I'm boring her on a brand-new level.

What the hell are you talking about, Towsey?

Anyhow, digressing slightly, the only real advice I'll offer in this section is to practice like hell while never losing a sense of your inner voice. Embrace that rawness that turned you to writing in the first place and try not to take on too much information (I guess that goes a little against the grain of what this book is about, but hey). If you try seeking perfection from the get-go, rigidity and linearity will become your worst enemy, and you'll just end up feeling overwhelmed.

Example…

My first ever horror story, 'Hugh's Friend,' was a cute(?) little tale about a boy and his invisible friend who constantly got them into all sorts of trouble (happy to send the original version to anyone who requests it). Knowing the story was a belter with one hell of a sucker punch ending; I couldn't wait to submit it. When 'Books N Pieces' picked it up for seventy-five dollars, the smile on my face lasted more than a week. But I look back at that story now and see all sorts of errors, not limited to run-ons and lousy sentence structure.

Do I regret putting it out there? No!

It's all part of the journey, and as some of you will know, the technical stuff is something we pick up in time. Simply the affirmation that I had the imagination for this racket kept me going and onto the next twisted tale. Since then, I've written over a hundred and fifty stories, many of which have sold at a pro-rate and connected me with some wonderful people. That's not a boast but an emphasis that the rest comes with practice. Beginners, please never fear putting pen to paper or having to tick boxes along the way. Imagination is your ticket for most of the way.

Short stories rock and are a fantastic sharpening tool for the skill set...

Although I've just finished my first novel, 'Chasing The Dragon,' I still have immense fondness for short stories. While allowing us authors to keep the tools sharp, they really are a quick fix if time is your enemy. And getting your short stories into anthologies is an excellent way of connecting with people in the industry and winning over readers who might not ordinarily have discovered your work. Perhaps more importantly, they're a chance to explore the emotions you are feeling at a specific point in time. You feel angry? Write a story about anger. You feel sad? Write a story about sadness. You feel homicidal? Write a story about... unicorns.

Writing is medicine, helping to heal my wounds and replenishing my shield. If you don't put this next quote on the book cover, Kevin, I'll be disappointed: Imagination is immunity from the demons lurking in the recesses of our minds.

Parting note on the writing industry...

Like in life, there are those I've encountered carrying negative energy, but the writing industry is primarily warm and receptive. As I'm in Australia, I don't get down to events or the chance to network as often as I would like. Still, I've had the pleasure of conversing with some wonderful people and working on collaborations with other cool authors such as Chisto Healy, Daemon Manx, and Erik Hanson. Getting to work with Kevin Kennedy has to be one of the biggest highlights of my career to date, though.

Cheesier than a cheese ball, Towsey.

Overall, I've learned a lot in the five years I've been writing. There are things I would do differently, including telling my early 'wet behind the ears' self to slow down a little, not necessarily from the point of view of writing the stories but where to market them. Be vigilant and do your research. Plenty of places glitter like gold but turn to black ash once contracts are signed.

Please don't do it for the money!

Aside from saving myself a fortune on therapy sessions, I'm not doing this for the money. And it's a bloody good job, to be honest. If that's your aim, to become an overnight success and watch your books get turned into box office movies, you need to slap yourself back into reality or get someone else to do it for you. Write for no other reason than to vanquish the demons that plague you, or on a lighter note, just for the sheer bloody fun of it.

Hey, Hi. You're Never Going to be Good Enough.
By
Mercedes M. Yardley

Ouch, that hurts. I hope you read the title of this essay and think, "What terrible advice! Who are you to say I'll never be good enough? Get bent, loser."

Good, my sweet, fellow writer. Let that rage build inside of you and keep you warm at night, because this industry can be tough. Writing is hard enough. Some of you try to find a quiet place to write. It's difficult because there's family or kids or roommates. Or you're so busy that eking out a few minutes to write seems nearly impossible. Or you're alone and the silence is overwhelming. Or perhaps you're depressed and can't muster up the energy, or you're too stressed and your head is full of fractured thoughts and pinpricks of light. No matter what your situation, writing itself can be a challenge.

The ideas. The working. Editing. Rethinking. Revising. Polishing up. Beta reading. Submitting.

Rinse and repeat.

You get better. You sell short stories, poems, articles, and essays. One day you're invited to your first anthology. You start seeing your names on book covers. You sell a novel or maybe two. You're working on a collaboration with an author you respect. You win awards. Some of them are even awards that Normies (i.e., people not in the horror world) have even heard of.

But you aren't done yet! Your book is optioned to be made into a movie. It becomes a movie. The movie is (or isn't) a hit and everybody learns it is based on your book. They flock to read it.

Isn't this heaven? Isn't this what you wanted? You're on podcasts and local shows and eventually worldwide. You're a guest of honor at international conferences! They put you up in a freakin' castle, for crying out loud, and you're writing and happy and the world is perfect, the end.

Except that isn't the end, at all. There's always more. More things you should be doing. More things you should be concentrating on. You wrote a book that became a best seller. Wonderful! Now you need to write another one, except it needs to be even more brilliant. It needs to be similar enough to your last one that it fits your brand, but not so similar that they call you a one-trick pony.

So, you need to do more writing. More marketing. You need to show up at more book signings and shake more hands. You won an award, but there's a better, more prestigious award to win. You need to do this. You need to do that.

No matter how wonderful your career is doing, you're never going to be good enough. The pressure will pile up and you'll become incapacitated and unable to write for a solid year. Trust me, I know this from personal experience. Responsibilities will weigh you down and you'll say, "Where is the fun in this? Didn't I begin writing because it was a joy? Part of my human makeup? If I am a writer, and I can no longer write, then who am I?"

It's a dark thought, and one I struggled with. Each milestone showed me that I was several steps behind many of contemporaries. Despite my successes, people expressed their disappointment that I hadn't accomplished more. The better I did, the worse I felt about myself.

Until I tried one brain hack that changed everything: Celebrate every success.

Celebrate every success. Every single one. That means celebrating when you get a personal rejection instead of a form one. Cheering when an agent asks for a partial instead of wondering why she didn't ask for the full manuscript. Be thrilled when you're asked to be on a panel at a conference, when you sell a short story even though your novel is still being shopped, and being happy when somebody reviews your book even if it isn't as glowing as you had hoped.

Every success is important. Every success matters. If you practice being present and excited now instead of worrying about the future, you'll find the literary process so much sweeter. You deserve to feel that satisfaction and joy now, so don't wait until later.

Let's celebrate.

Writer's Firsts of a Long Journey
By
Eric J. Guignard

Ah, the world of indie horror. The *wild* world of indie horror. Not for the faint of heart, to be sure. It's a world of thrills, chills, and buzz-kills. A world of emotions, too, certainly—so prepare yourself for tears of frustration as well as leaps of jubilant joy; this is, after all, a world of passion, and nobody is more passionate about this world than its own creator (i.e. now, you, this newest world-purveyor!). Where I'm going with this analogy is that it's a different experience for everybody, and the world of indie horror is as much a sum of your peers' experiences as it is for how you mold it to fit yourself.

For my own experience, I've been writing fiction with publication since February, 2011. I was 35 years old at the time, and in hindsight I wish I'd pursued writing when I was younger. I'd written and illustrated stories ever since I was a child, although I'd only done it previously for my own interest or for friends. I stopped in college, in order to pursue business and serious-minded life necessities, which I now regret. I don't regret the pursuit of those other things, but I regret having given up writing for so many years. I never went to school for writing, and I only jumped into it as a potential career-type desire after the realization struck me that I was missing out on something I'd been passionate about before, and had been stuck in these other job cycles related to endeavors that gave me no enjoyment or enthusiasm.

But no sour grapes, as such is life. At the time of my writing this, it's been about twelve years since I set foot into the world of indie horror. A lot has happened in those years, personally, and in terms of the industry. Tastes, technology, trying times, and triumphs, too (nice alliteration, right?). I've published much, won some awards, made many, MANY friends (truly a reward of its own), maybe some enemies, too (don't dwell on it though), and endured the proverbial roller coaster of this profession.

Now I have knowledge. When I started, I did not. I had presumptions. Expectations. Beliefs. And reality hit me hard in each regard, but I have carried on. Perseverance in this game is key, and I say that with the utmost sincerity and conviction.

Herein, a few anecdotes, or "Writer's Firsts of a Long Journey":

When I first wanted to publish a short story, this happened:
When I started writing with purpose, all I

wanted was to get a story published. So I wrote a few tales that were promising, and picked out the best of them, and I sent it out to a publisher. Said publisher was *Weird Tales* (back then, a massive, massive name and force in the industry—fingers crossed, it's coming back under Jonathan Maberry's helm). Incredibly, I then announced to family and friends I was going to be published there, to join company in the same magazine that had published H.P. Lovecraft, Tennessee Williams, Robert E. Howard, et. al.

Had I actually been accepted by *Weird Tales*? No. Why did I tell people I was going to be published there, when I had only merely submitted? Because I had a disconnect in my mind about the submission process. I thought magazines published pretty much anybody who sent them work. I was so naïve about the process that I believed my first horror story would prove to be an immediate acceptance because it was brilliant. I mean, my confidence had been that *Weird Tales* would love my writing so much, they'd make me a regular contributor or, at the least, I'd get cover story status.

The rejection letter that arrived stung. And now I consider that what I'd sent was such a silly piece of banal religious horror anyway, that not even the most odious of bad presses has ever offered to publish it since (i.e. it remains unsold, in the deepest of my trunk drawers). Also, as I later learned, *Weird Tales* was getting something like three or four thousand submissions a month, and they would only buy a couple stories from that slush pile, outside what they solicited from authors they wanted to work with.

But I dried my tears, and wrote something else, and I resubmitted to all the big markets, and they all rejected me, and then I did due diligence and tried to figure out for the first time who would actually be a good partner, and not just aim for the biggest name on the bookstore shelf. Eventually I found an indie press, and they published my first short story, and then they promptly went out of business.

I was forever thus "a published writer."

When I first wanted to join a writer's group, this happened:

I looked online for groups local to me. I found one and made my inquiry, and they told me there was a membership fee. For an online writer's group? Turned out, it was just a guy hiring himself out as an overpriced "pay-for-critique" service, in which his random clients constituted his "writer's group."

Second time I tried to join a group, I went to a neighboring city, where they had a monthly meeting at a small library. I attended, and the people were sweet. It was mostly elderly folks working on memoirs (nothing wrong with that, but I wanted to discuss genre fiction), and a couple who regularly "talked about the books they were going to write" rather than actually doing any writing. One gentleman gave me a business card that claimed he was a "best-selling author," only there was a misspelling and he'd written it as "auther" (not in an ironic way). It wasn't a good fit for me.

I tried a couple of other writing groups and, like dating, they didn't work out for different reasons. Then I discovered the Horror Writers Association (HWA), the largest international group dedicated to horror literature, and I realized that I had found my people. I love HWA, and I've been a member since 2012, and they've been instrumental in my development in the horror genre. I recommend the group to any aspiring horror author. Yes, there is a fee for membership, but the services and connections returned (at least to me), have been invaluable.

When I first wanted to edit an anthology, this happened:

This probably won't apply to most readers of this book who are aspiring authors.

But I'm a short story lover at heart, and I was

influenced deeply by horror anthologies of the 1990s (*Whispers*, ed. by Stuart David Schiff; *Borderlands*, ed. by Thomas Monteleone; *Masques*, ed. by J.N. Williamson, etc.), and I desired to edit my own anthology. Two reasons: I wanted to become a better writer by understanding what it was to acquire, edit, and distribute material; and I also wanted to emulate projects that I loved, to pay it forward by promoting other writers of the genre.

Because I had no partnership with a press, this endeavor became much like short story submissions. I wrote to publishers with my pitch idea, and they rejected me (or ignored me completely). A few asked, "What authors would I bring to them?" but I had none. So simultaneously, I began reaching out to authors and asked if they would commit to submitting a story to me based on my idea of horror mixed with ancient kingdoms, to be titled *Dark Tales of Lost Civilizations*. Most authors weren't interested because I had no anthology experience and that I had no publisher partnership. But publishers wouldn't partner with me because I was a nobody (and they would do anthologies in-house anyway) and that I didn't have any authors who would yet work with me.

Chicken and egg scenario. In football parlance, I pulled a Hail Mary. I begged around, got a P.O. Box address for an author I adored, being Joe R.

Lansdale, and blindly asked if he would participate. He agreed, at a price, and only because he was in between projects (and if you don't know him, he's a wildly prolific writer, so that was a providential fluke). I then resubmitted my pitches to more indie presses, and one day a random one responded that they too were a fan of Lansdale, and maybe we could talk, if my promise of bringing in a Lansdale story was true. It almost didn't happen, and there was a lot of begging and pleading involved, and I had to finance the anthology myself, and I did all the work on it, but that press was Dark Moon Books, and its owner was Stan Swanson, and he became a dear mentor of the process as well as an invaluable source of wisdom and guidance thereafter, of which I am eternally grateful.

Had it not been for Lansdale's name though, I probably never would have found a press to give me a chance to start putting together anthologies, which to this day is still a substantial passion (and of which, I will always proclaim, has truly made me a much better writer).

When I first wanted to explore paid marketing, this happened:

There are lots of companies and individuals who, for a fee, will promote your work through any number of advertising channels or marketing approaches, including tons of book promo sites and big-name review-for-hire companies. I've always heard that you have to invest money into your product to expand. So I explored how best to pay for promotions of my first anthology while on a very miniscule budget. I hired a P.R. blogger who claimed to be able to increase book sales. I paid her money. She quickly absconded, never to be heard from again.

And my book sales did not increase.

(*There are many reputable sites to trust in such business, and I've since engaged the services of a few ((never to any great personal success)), but the lesson is to do due diligence in advance, find former customers who give them good reviews.)

When I first wanted to set up an author signing for myself, this happened:

I envisioned a bookstore, in which I'd sit behind a table filled with stacks of my publications, promotional material, and maybe a large banner declaring me somewhat of a minor celebrity. There'd be food and drink, good conversation. Additionally there would be a very long line of fans, each breathlessly clutching a copy of something I'd been involved with, and eager to speak with me, while I scrawled for hours the old John Hancock.

Admittedly, the first part occurred as I'd

dreamed. I got to have a signing at the largest horror-themed bookstore in Los Angeles called Dark Delicacies. (If you're ever in the area, go visit them—they're tireless advocates of horror at all levels.) I would not have been allowed to sign by myself, but Dark Delicacies had (still have) "shared signings" where multiple authors sign alongside each other. I had a story in an anthology with a few other Los Angeles locals who had much more credibility than myself, and I was allowed to come along with them one afternoon. So the bookstore had a table for me, although I had to bring in my own books (i.e. they wouldn't stock them on the shelves), and I sat on the end of 5 or 6 other authors.

    I advertised myself in advance, made flyers, shouted it out on social media, but I quickly realized not a single person would have come to see me if I had been on my own. I got to sign books because some customers bought the anthology based on the strength of the other authors, and figured, "What the hell, may as well have the newbie sign, too." The best part of the signing though was getting to know the other authors who'd all been good people, supportive, friendly, and had much experience that they were willing to share, and I'm still working alongside them in publications today.

When I first wanted to promote myself at a

library, this happened:

I'd learned my lesson from that first book signing—Don't try to sign books alone. Do it with others and share the stage. I got a great idea to create a promotions event at a large city library in Pasadena. It was: "Panel Discussions on the Topic of Horror Fiction, Along With Readings and Book Signings by Local Authors!"

I set it up: The library let us use their auditorium to speak and we had a nice garden area to sign. It was a beautiful venue. We were scheduled to be there three hours.

There were seven of us authors. No one else came for the event. Not one person.

When I first received a royalties check, this happened:

It was for approximately $1.42. That's one dollar and forty-two cents, real United States currency. Since then, sometimes the money I make writing fiction is more, sometimes less. I have to work a day-job like most other writers and artists. It's a tough (and lucky) road to get to a place where you can subsist purely on the money made from creative endeavors. I know some writers who do it, but it's a low percentage. And there's no guarantee of a continuance from one year to the next. For those writers who *do* find high-level success, I was told by several people that it takes at least ten years of writing novels to hopefully reach that place. Maybe one day it will happen for me. Maybe one day it will happen for you, too. In the meantime, I pay my bills as a corporate Technical Writer.

When I first received a wonderful book review:

I shouted with joy, leapt up from my desk, told the world—someone loved my book!!! It was uplifting, but then I went back to writing my next piece. The review did not affect my book sales.

When I first received a terrible book review:

I survived. I didn't like it, but I asked around and never encountered a single reputable source who ever said every person will like your work. It's part of the business. And the review did not affect my book sales.

When I first went to a writer's convention:

The first writer's convention I went to was World Horror Con in Salt Lake City, Utah, 2012. I didn't know anybody, aside from a few social media interactions and conversations in chat rooms. I stood by myself a lot of the con. It was awkward, and I felt like I didn't belong. But I forced myself to interact, to introduce myself to strangers, and after that it got easier—they weren't strangers anymore, and I've come to see a lot of the same people at convention after convention, year after year, and now consider them dear friends.

When I first wanted to publish a novel, this happened:

It took me about five years to write my first full-length novel *Doorways to the Deadeye*. I'd been feeling a weird imposter syndrome that people wouldn't take me seriously if I was only a short story writer and couldn't accomplish a longer work. But I published the novel, and my life didn't change, and I realized that I still liked writing short stories better instead. Plus my novel publishing experience was sort of a letdown—I had a falling-out with the indie publisher, and no one was there to market this book except for me, which got to be an exhausting time-suck. I received wonderful blurbs from writer friends and glowing reviews, but once a book has been out for a couple months, it's time to move onto something else anyway. I do recognize that there's a greater chance of success in the industry that's driven by novels, and I'm working on a few others, but I can't—and don't want to—get away from my passion. I've published over a hundred short stories in Horror and Dark Fantasy (HDF) markets around the world so far, and hope to put out several hundred more.

When I first wanted to set up an indie press, this happened:

I discovered that Dark Moon Books, where I'd published my first anthology, had essentially gone out of business.

I was interested in learning more about writing from the publishing side, to be able to have full control over book design, placement, distribution, and so I spoke with its owner, Stan Swanson, and we negotiated a price, and I bought out the company. The deal sounds bigger than it was—essentially all I was buying was the publishing name and the website, which had been taken over by spammers. But I now owned a publishing company, and I completely rebranded it. I dropped all of its former titles, built out a new secure website and logo, and set a goal for it to be a short story venue, primarily for anthologies and my own passion projects which wouldn't work elsewhere. My mission statement is for "Dark Moon Books to publish unusual and invigorating dark fiction for readers around the world."

It's been a bitter-sweet experience, and I'm immensely proud of it, but if I had to go back in time, I wouldn't do it again. I've learned invaluable lessons from running a small press, and can now put out quality books when I want, and with full control over them. But for the amount of time and cost I put into them, each is a financial loss. Yet since I've spent the grueling years of learning it, I'm at the point I can easily keep doing it, for whenever inspiration and ambition strike.

The biggest problem I discovered is that I wanted to run a small press for the sake of wisdom, and—like editing anthologies—with the belief it would make me a better writer, which it has. Unfortunately that amount of time I spend in publishing takes away from the time I'd have had for writing, so I don't get the writing done that I wanted to, when under self-imposed commitment for publishing and design projects.

When I first decided to write this article, this happened:

I originally planned for this article to be only about 1,200 words, but it's grown to three times that length, because it's been a pleasant and contemplative trip down such Memory Lane. Writing is a journey, albeit a long and winding one (and generally without any certain destination), and something that is unique to every individual.

In closing, consider that I've shared with you a number of my firsts. But know that each of those first events leads to a second, and a third, and so on, and each occurrence is easier and more assuring than the one before, and suddenly you're well on your own personal writing journey. Every once in a awhile, look back and consider those firsts: If you haven't already, soon you will have your first publication credit, your first reading, your first networking event, and by those aggregate of experiences will you find your own place in the World of Indie Horror.

Time Is A River That Is Sometimes Still
By
John Boden

I'm going to ramble a bit about time. You all know what time is, I know. But the notion that there's an expiration date on success or doing things. That kinda time.

See, when I was in high school, I wanted to be a writer. I had already been in love with the works of Bradbury, King and others and I had been cranking out awful pastiche type stories and passing them around to my friends. I wanted to do it for real. I wanted to mail them to a publisher and get a letter back saying how much they liked them. I wanted to be a real honest to God author. I also thought that meant I had to be a teacher of some kind. All the authors I liked seemed to have landed in that position so I thought it was part of the deal. I graduated high school and tawdled off to college I couldn't afford and failed out after two years. I did well in my English and writing classes, everything else was abysmal. I quit and moved back home for a few months before moving out on my own, as a grown up, for good.

During all of this I still wrote. Scraps of stories and poetry all of it went right from my manual typewriter into a box where it stayed. Eventually, I stopped doing even that. Life arched its back and raised its fur, took me in its teeth and shook....I got a job, I got married, I had kids, I forgot all about the writing stuff. For almost a dozen years.

In 2009, my friend, Ken Wood and I were chatting. We had met on a CD trading site and were fellow metalheads and so we connected on that and lots of other stuff...so when he got the idea to start a horror fiction magazine, like the old *CREEPY* and *EERIE* ones, he wanted me to come on board and assist. I jumped at the chance. We asked another friend, Nick Contor on and then a 4th. The fourth staffer usually ending up like a drummer for *SPINAL TAP,* which means they never lasted. We finally found a permanent fourth after publication of the first issue of *SHOCK TOTEM*. Yeah, that was what we settled on for a name. We asked a new author, Mercedes Yardley to join us and she agreed and together we all (mostly...some folks dropped off and others stepped in but the core of the staff was the four of us for most of it) delivered almost a dozen issues of the digest. Quite well received issues stuffed with new voices in dark fiction, several who went on the much bigger things, others never were heard from again. That's the way.

    I say all that to say that reading those submissions awoke the dormant desire in me to write. And so I started again. And with the support of peers and new friends in the genre, I started sending things out, often met with rejection. Until I landed my first acceptance, a short flash piece that ran on a blog called 52 STITCHES, run by Aaron Poulson. After that I had a few more acceptances...slowly building to the point where I was just cocky enough to try a novella. I had by that point, realized that traditional narrative and style was not for me. Thus I knew the subject would need to be uniquely something I could hold close and nurture in my purple prose-ian way. I went with a Coming-of-Age story. I wrote a semi-autobiographical one about me and my little brother and the summer I was thirteen. It went well. It's been through several printings and publishers, most recent being Cemetery Dance. I've since written several other books. Solo and with collaborators. Each one slowly built my confidence in my writing. But at the same time, it is perfectly normal to be terrified that you suck and/or that the whole thing is a fluke that you'll be discovered for. Impostor Syndrome is real and not kind.

So what the hell am I jabbering about? You have all the time in the world. You have as much time as you need to do what you want. I allowed almost 20 years of inactivity to flow from my high school tenacity to when I really started to try it on for real. I often think of what might've happened had I not done that? Could I be a big name author now? Maybe but that line of thought is as dangerous as others. Just take hold of the now and do what you feel led to do. Don't dog yourself for waiting or being too old or too young or not good enough. Don't fret over a degree or lack of degree or any of that. Just do it. When you want and how you want. Keep it honest. Keep it real. *–John Boden*

Learning to Write Happy
By
Alex Laybourne

All I ever wanted to do was be a gangster writer. My earliest memories involve reading books and writing stories. Now, at the age of 38, well, most likely 39, by the time you read this, I can stand up and say that I am a full-time writer. I am living my dream life. However, it wasn't all plain sailing, and even now, it's different from the writer's life I had imagined.

I was nervous when Kevin asked me if I wanted to contribute a non-fiction story to this wonderful anthology. I didn't know what I was going to say. If I'm honest with myself, I've not done anything special with my writing, and a lot of what I've written wasn't my best work, as it was written when I was anything but myself. So I figured maybe a tale of my journey and how it masked my personal struggles may help others somehow. Perhaps it's just a story I needed to tell and found a possible outlet for.

Only time will tell, I guess.

My first novel was published in 2011, a fact which is, in and of itself, a terrifying reminder of the unyielding passage of time. I was over the moon when a publisher said they wanted to publish my book and the next two in the proposed trilogy.

I also found myself growing roots in the online horror community at the time. I was chatting with Joe Mynhardt when he opened the doors to Crystal Lake Publishing. A company I knew was destined for big things from day one. I connected with people and dove headfirst into writing, well on the road to becoming the worst possible version of myself, with my stories being the perfect masking device.

In the following years, my writing hit several snags, including four different publishers who ended up conning or scamming me somehow. I also made several mistakes, some more than once. I don't dwell on it. Things happen, and we live and grow as a result. I continued to write, and thanks to my friend and fellow author Eric S. Brown, I was introduced to Severed Press. A pulp horror publisher based in Australia. I started writing quicker and quicker, churning out stories about monsters and beasts faster than I had any right to. Looking back now, I know it wasn't my best writing, but I was still drowning in my life, and writing was the main thing keeping me afloat, much to my detriment. For years I wrote from behind a wall, a safe place I had created. I started writing because I loved to write, but somewhere along the way, I began to write in an attempt to hide. I told myself a long-running lie: everything was alright because I was writing.

Then, in 2020, the world changed. Life changed for everybody thanks to COVID-19, but for me, it changed in more ways than one.

To start off the year, my grandfather, a man who was my best friend, died. A few weeks prior, I travelled over from Holland to say goodbye. He had been in the hospital for months, and when I got there, he couldn't really talk, and during my time with him, he rarely woke. Yet, for a split second, when it was just me and him, he opened his eyes, looked right at me, and in a moment of unimaginable clarity, said, "Hello, sport!" He said nothing more after that but drifted back into the haze.

That night, in a lightbulb moment, I realized that my self-sabotaging ways were my attempts to mask a deep depression. I realized I would never see my best friend again. It still eats away at me that I allowed someone to control my life so extremely that I hadn't seen my grandfather in several years. Everything unravelled the deep unhappiness that was eating away at me. Writing was how I coped. For years I buried myself in my books, churning out word after word, story upon story. Many of which will never see the light of day. I wrote because I loved to write, but I also wrote because it allowed me to escape. I found solace in my stories for as long as I was writing; I could ignore the harsh reality I didn't want to face.

The moment of clarity I had when saying goodbye to my grandfather was incredibly sobering, an experience, unlike anything I have ever felt before. In all honesty, I hope I never have to feel it again. Throughout the rest of the year, my life turned upside down. I got divorced, I moved back to the UK, and along the way, I stopped doing what I loved, and it bothered me. I wanted to write, but try as I might, I couldn't.

We all know that covid changed the world in 2020, and it was easy for me to blame that on my lack of writing and, but this point also, reading. It had been months since I touched a book. The ideas were there. They were always there, but I just couldn't bring myself to put pen to paper. The few times I tried, it resulted in nothing—a few thousand words here or a hundred. Nothing ever stuck. It was as if I had somehow forgotten how to write. I had experienced lulls in my writing, but never anything like this. The thing I found strangest of all was that I was actually happy. I wanted to write. I was desperate to write again, but in all other areas of my life, I was actually happy. Looking back now, I realize that if I'm honest, I have never been happy before. Not consistently, not even as a child. There were moments, holidays with my grandparents, but on the whole, happiness had always eluded me.

Then, one day, I was out in the pub with a few friends after our weekly D&D game got cancelled for the evening, and they pointed it out to me. I had spent so many years using my writing as a way of hiding from the world and writing to create my own little place of happiness; I just didn't know how to write when I was happy. Of course, they said this mostly in jest, poking fun at the whole tortured artist stereotype. However, they were right. I didn't need to write as a way to escape my own world anymore.

I loved where I was and who I was.

For the first time, I had a circle of friends, and I could go out and have a few drinks in the evening. I had started tabletop gaming and was elbow-deep in

Dungeons and Dragons campaigns; I enjoyed being at home and spending time with my fiancee. In short, I had a great life.

Around this time, I was made redundant from my job of eleven years. Again, in a rather obtuse twist of the normal, I was ecstatic about this and didn't even wait for them to finish talking before I accepted their severance offer. Working in an office was not for me, and never had been.

So, with a young family, a new mortgage, and no job, I sat down one evening and spoke things through with my fiancee. I told her that I wanted to try and write full-time. I had written freelance articles in my spare time for some years but never envisioned taking this step. Yet, something inside of me was screaming that it's-now-or-never alarm that bellowed hard enough to keep me awake at night. Could I really take that risk? Should I? I didn't care. I had the chance, and within a few weeks of pitching and applying for writing tasks, I landed a steady gig writing for a website, and I was off.

I was actually writing every day. Day in, day out, just my big butt in a seat hammering out the words. Fast forward 18 months, and I am still going. I'm supporting the family with my words, and I can proudly say I hold the number 1 spot on Google for a significant number of articles on various topics.

A year and a half of writing full-time has taught me a lot. However, I have yet to write much fiction. I wrote a short story for an anthology recently. I wasn't accepted, but the feedback was good, and I felt great for starting and finishing a complete story. Thankfully, the ideas are flowing freely. They feel substantial for the first time in a long while, branching out from abstract concepts into full outlines. What's next? I have an exciting opportunity coming up to write for a video game, another dream I have long held onto. I am also working on a short story for an anthology from the wonderful publisher that brought you his book.

It has taken a long time, but I am slowly teaching myself how to write while happy and can sit back and smile at the brightness of my horizon.

Memoirs of an Indie Idiot
By
Adam Millard

I became a full-time author in 2010. After a dozen years of welding and grinding, and drilling, and taking extended breaks on the toilet in which I could jot down plotlines and character notes for the evening of writing that lay ahead, I sold my first novel, and immediately—somewhat recklessly, some might say—informed the foreman of my decision to lay down tools, wash my grimy face for the very last time, and where he was to shove my welding torch for the many years of pressure, seventy-eight hour weeks, and smarmy remarks about my choice of haircut.

I was, or so I believed, free of the manual pain and toil that came with a regular job. From now on it would be all hotels, and sold-out book signings, at which there would be lines of obsequious fans clutching my books to their chest as if it were the most important publication since *The Bible*, Shelley's *Frankenstein*, or whichever book featuring a bespectacled wizard was popular at that time, before Rowling went all nuts on us and it was okay to start calling people "four-eyes" again.

I would sell out readings, just like my peers, and I'd be able to drink like Bukowski, fuck like

Bukowski, fight like Bukowski, and when I wasn't drinking and fighting and fucking, the publishers would come to me! They would fight over the rights to my next novel in those auctions that you're always hearing about but never invited to.

I was it. I was the man. I was, as we say in Blighty, sorted.

My first novel sold just over one thousand copies, which wasn't bad considering its limited print-run. However, I understand that the unsold copies were remaindered, which meant that the pages had been torn from them and sent to Africa to be used as toilet paper, or something…

My dream was over before it had even started. Adam Millard was a hack, a one-hit wonder, and not only that but I'd burnt my bridges as a fabricator/welder and told the foreman to shove my torch where the sun didn't shine, which in hindsight was a silly thing to do, and an even sillier thing for him to obey.

I had a few choices, of which none seemed appealing at the time. Money was running out quickly from the sales of my first novel. In fact, I think it was all gone before its release. Turns out that writing is an expensive profession, once you factor in the cost of all the whiskey, the ink cartridges, the whiskey, the printing paper, and the whiskey. So, my choices were as follows:

1) Admit I may have jumped the gun a little and pop on down to the JobCentre. Get myself another welding job, and admit that my fifteen minutes of fame were, in fact, only eight minutes, and that was if you included a tea break.

2) Kill myself, which I didn't fancy at the time because I was still scared of heights after my short career in the Parachute Regiment, and drinking myself to death was far too expensive, since I'd built up a ridiculous tolerance to alcohol as a burgeoning writer and now only fifteen litres of bleach could possibly put a dent in my organs.

3) Keep writing, keep submitting, keep on trucking.

And so, it was option three for me. I did just that, and I have written and have had published over forty novels, twenty novellas, and two hundred-ish short stories. I became a writer, one just about successful enough to pay the bills, one good enough to be included in top-ten lists occasionally. One funny enough to have been compared to Pratchett, Adams, Rankin, and thankfully never Rowling.

I became I writer.

And that's where the fun began.

The Authors, the Hotel, The Champagne and the Vomit

I founded Crowded Quarantine Publications in 2011, with the help of all the money I was making from my short stories and royalties (at least £13.27 per month), and quickly gathered a roster of impressive talent from across the world willing to take a chance on a small independent press from the UK. I won't name them all here, because this is my article and they should all know by now that nothing is free in this world, not even a mention.

I published dozens of authors, some just starting out in the business and some veterans, and it was a wonderful time. We had successful anthologies such as Of Devils and Deviants (2014) and Grindhouse (2012), and I'm proud to say that when CQP closed its doors a few years ago, no royalty statement or payment had ever been late, no animosity had ever arisen between us and our authors, and when the business ran its course, I had the same amount of money as when it began.

Zero.

The memories that were made over the course of those eight years were all that mattered, which brings me to this wonderful little anecdote featuring a relatively small cast of characters who I shall name, because they're going to pay me later, as it should be. The problem with this story is that there should have been a helluva bigger cast list, as you shall discover.

In my infinite wisdom as one of the greatest up-and-coming writers on the indie scene (their words, not mine) and with a publishing company to boot, which was the holy duality—I was still waiting for the Holy Spirit to show up—there was only one thing to do. I would create… an event. An *event* the likes of which had never been seen before, an evening of marvel and mystery, of spectacle and suspense. I invited three of the best authors I knew, and when they turned me down, I sent messages to Rich Hawkins, Craig Saunders, and Joseph Freeman, all of which had been around the block a bit by then and probably needed a good night out anyway. Unsurprisingly, they all said yes—of *course* they did, *I* was going to be there—and so we each descended upon a large, yet scarcely populated, hotel in the middle of Fuckknowswhere, just a few hundred yards from Nopestillnobodyhere.

I had spent a lot of money on marketing the event, which just goes to show that carrier pigeons don't work too well in this day and age, no matter how cheap they are, and as a treat for everyone in attendance, there was champagne. Lots of champagne, probably too much champagne, if I'm being perfectly honest, but it seemed like a good idea at the time.

There we were. Myself, Hawkins, Saunders, Freeman, and our respective better halves, except I don't think mine was there that night, which was probably for the best or our doomed marriage might have ended even sooner than it did. We were all filled with excitement as we glanced around the well-presented conference room, the hundreds of empty seats staring back us like seats with eyes, the waft of freshly poured champagne lingering in the air like butterfly farts, and we waited and discussed our future projects, and waited and talked about our latest acceptances in various magazines and anthologies, and waited... and waited...

It soon became very apparent that nobody was coming, and the only thing left to do was not allow all that champagne to go to waste. However, I had already been let loose on the house Merlot, and after the disappointment of such a poor turnout, I looked to the carpet and thought, "Such a bland colour. Far too white. Let me fix that for you."

I fixed about two square metres of it with my Merlot puke before a harried staff member ran in with what I can only assume was a bucket, but I had drunk so much it might very well have been a tortoise shell or an off-duty policeman's helmet. I was ashamed, of course, but I was more disappointed for my authors, for their wives, and for the poor woman now carrying half a turtle of Merlot across the room, trying not to spill any. It was a shock ending to an otherwise fun night, and that's what being an indie author is about.

The Airport Contraband (Piss, Dildos. and Knives, oh my!!)

One of the great things about being an author is the travel. I love seeing new places, meeting the locals, and tasting exotic foods. You can't beat it. That is, until about two days into the trip when you've had just about enough of being mocked for your accent and you just want to get home to a nice egg sandwich and a bath where the water spins the correct way down the plughole.

One trip in 2015 had me so excited. I would be travelling to America for the very first time. Not only that, but I would be spending five days at BizarroCon, the leading Bizarro writing convention in the world, where I would meet all of my favourite authors, many of whom I'd been friends or acquaintances with on social media for many years. It was a dream come true, and I would make the most of it.

What followed was a magnificent festival of the bizarre, readings that would make Anthony Jeselnik wince, wonderful music and amazing performances from pretty much everyone who had registered for the event. It was a very special long weekend, one that will live in my mind until the moment I die.

However, what will also live in my mind until the moment I die is the return trip to England. You see, while I was at BizarroCon, I participated in The Ultimate Bizarro Showdown, a competition to give the most entertaining, weirdest performance possible in under three minutes, and as I am both weird and entertaining (their words, not mine) I signed up. Fortunately, I had a plan.

I would read humorous and silly lines... whilst being waxed. Yes, not really weird by today's standards, but you'd never see Virginia Woolf doing it.

The performance went well. So well, in fact, I won a consolation prize, which just so happened to be a dildo fist molded from the very famous adult actress, Belladonna. And so proud was I of this trophy, I wanted to get it home. I had won it, after all, it was mine, all mine, and it would live in infamy on my bookshelf next to all the empty spaces where there would later be Stokers or FantasyCons, or Nebulas.

I packed it in my suitcase and headed off to the airport following a very successful convention, which was only phase one of where I'd gone wrong on that fateful return trip to the UK. Phase two was me forgetting to use the toilet before leaving

McMenamins, the convention hotel, and we were still several miles from the airport with my bladder already spilling over. I had no choice.

"Is there a toilet we can stop at around here?" I asked the cab driver, feeling a little like a child and yet not caring.

"Just piss into this," he said, handing an empty bottle to me over his shoulder. "Just don't leave it in the back of the cab when you get out."

I was a little taken aback by this as I accepted the bottle, not because of the driver's nonchalant attitude toward me attempting to urinate into a one-inch-hole in the back of his cab, but the thought that this happened so often, he would open the back doors of an evening and hundreds of piss-bottles would just fall out.

After managing to get most of the urine into the bottle—I say most because there are very few rules of the road in the US, and certainly none to slow a cab driver down just because his passenger's slashing into a Fanta bottle—I stashed the bottle in my suitcase as we approached the airport.

That was the last I thought about it until, two hours later, I was standing in front of a woman asking me if I'd packed the case myself as she slowly unzipped it. Before she had a chance to speak, I said, "It's just piss," which was an acceptable explanation to me in that moment, but not when she took out the fifteen-inch fist dildo first, which probably required more of an explanation than the piss.

"I won that," I informed her, somewhat nervously. "It's a trophy, and I won it."

"Uh-huh," she grunted, as did the thirty or so people standing in line behind me. She set it back down in the suitcase and finally came out with the piss bottle. "Can you dispose of it, please? No more than 100ml of liquid allowed on this flight."

As I shuffled past the thirty snickering commuters with a bottle of piss in my hand toward the receptacle at the end of the line, I thought to myself, *This is perhaps the funniest thing ever, and one day I'll have the balls to write it down and get it published.* So here you go. You're very welcome.

The knife at Birmingham airport was less funny. I was traveling to Glasgow to perform a reading and sign books at a sold-out event, and had almost made it through security when I was summoned to the naughty-step and informed of a Bear Grylls lock-knife in my jacket pocket which had been caught on its way through the scanner. I was in shock, because I knew why it was there, but not why I had forgotten to take it out following the previous weekend's mushroom foraging expedition in the West Midlands. How remiss of me. You would have thought I might have learned something from the piss-bottle episode in Portland, OR.

Fortunately, they accepted my story and allowed me to continue my journey, *sans* illegal foraging knife, and once again I had a story to tell, and a moral to pass on, and that moral is this:

An author will pass through many airports in their life, and naturally our lives are so inexplicably different in comparison to normal people, so always, always throw your piss out before you go through customs, always get a receipt for the strange sex trophies you acquire along the way, and learn to forage with a plastic spoon.

The Santapede Lawyer

In 2014, I wrote a short, festive novel parodying the successful horror film, *The Human Centipede*. I wrote *Vinyl Destination, Zoonami, Jurassic Car Park*, and I do this because, as an indie writer, I can parody the hell out of anything I like without repercussions. I know this because I am smart, and smart people never lie. Or because I read once that: *According to the court, for the parody exception to apply the work must (i) "evoke an existing work, while being noticeably different from it", and (ii) "constitute an expression of humour or mockery".*

Well, I did both with *The Human Santapede*, and it was warmly received by my constant readers (I apologise, Mr. King, but you can't trademark everything) and newcomers to my work alike. The main element was there; the ass-to-mouth crochet, but mine was a Christmas story, a wonderfully festive tale of Good versus Evil, Santa versus Krampus, elves sleeping with Santa's wife, who just happened to be the best pole-dancer in the, ahem, North Pole. The story was, like all good viruses, so widely spread that I received emails and messages of support from Tom Six, the director of *The Human Centipede*, and its star Dieter Laser. I even struck up a friendship with Laurence R. Harvey, the star of its sequel, and have the sex photos to prove it, and so I believed everything to be a-okay, "peachy in Finland" or whatever the opposite of "rotten in Denmark" actually is.

Years passed. I grew old, there were many great wars, presidents came and went and one of my legs fell off, when all of a sudden, I received a rather terse and insistent email from one of the guys at Six Productions. "You owe us royalties!" it said. "How very dare you use this premise for your novel. You're a nobody, a hack, and we will not rest until we have taken your children and your house from you, or you could just give us the two years' worth of royalties that you owe us."

Remember the cab incident from the previous story? Well, on this occasion I couldn't contain my bladder and I did, whilst laughing out loud and frightening the dog in the process, wet myself. It was hilarious to me that they, a production company, did not know the exemptions of parody and satire when it came to intellectual property. I had not copied the story verbatim, nor even come close. To begin with, theirs did not have a Santa in it, or a stripper Mrs. Claus, or a gaggle—I don't know what the collective noun is—of horny elves. I had won before I'd even started, which was a good thing because I didn't know of a good lawyer and barely had enough money to publish its sequel, *The Human Santapede II: This Time There are Thousands of Elves.*

I replied to the email from Six Productions with the same tone and brevity of their missive.

"Parody and satire. I owe you nothing."

Unsurprisingly, I didn't receive a response, and my novel is still on sale today, which leads me to believe that there are many people out there willing to take a chance on shutting down indie writers like myself, for we are many, we are Legion, and we are not restricted by the same rules as solely traditionally published authors. The extreme horror market is thriving, and many of these books would not see the light of day or even pass an agent's desk if they were not self-published or put out by an independent press.

Never let the so-called "big dogs" try to get you down. As long as you are writing, you are just as much of a writer as anyone. Except Stephanie Meyer.

You're already better than that.

"Never Meet Your Heroes"

This is not true. You should meet all of them when the opportunity presents itself, however, don't expect them to be as agreeable as you have imagined them to be. As an indie author, or anyone that has to work the convention scene to make a living, you will find yourself amongst the famous, those people you grew up with on the TV and within your chosen genre. You will, if you are fortunate enough for sales purposes, be seated beside one of the many great Doctors from *Doctor Who*, but it is far more likely that you will find yourself tabling next to another indie author, or that kid who was in the background at Hogwarts once, you know? The one with the gown on and the wand?

I had the privilege of sitting around a dinner table with the entire cast of *Red Dwarf* once, and I was awestruck. I did, in fact, feel like a smeg-head as I sat there and snuffled down tepid convention pizza as they laughed and discussed their business. Then the great Robert Llewellyn (Kryten) held aloft my recalcitrant child for a photo opportunity, much like Mufasa and Simba from *The Lion King*, and my day, and many great memories, were made instantly. We returned to our respective tables and continued to flog our wares as equals, even though his queue was ten times longer than mine and I didn't have people bringing me complimentary sandwiches and coffee every thirty minutes.

As an author I have met far more wonderful actors and writers than I could have ever imagined. Heather Langenkamp, Jsu Garcia, Warwick Davis, Robert Patrick, Tuesday Knight, Tony Todd, most or all of the Cenobites, pretty much everyone from Star Wars, lots of Doctor Whos, and hundreds upon hundreds of amazing writers and authors, both independently- and traditionally-published. It is one of the most delightful parts of the job. So yes, meet as many of your heroes as possible, but also bear in mind:

Some of them might turn out to be cunts.

Measuring Success as an Indie Author

The mileage of success will vary from author to author. For some, writing is all that matters, whether they turn out a thousand words a day or ten, whether they sell a story on the first attempt, or fail a few times at submission and hold it back for a future self-published collection. For others, success is making that first pro-rate sale, or being accepted into HWA, or being nominated for an award, or being invited to an anthology that they hadn't even heard of by an editor they didn't even know acknowledged their existence. For some, it is determined by the ability to create time to do other things, such as: *if I write and sell this novel, I can take a break for three months, visit Grandma before she dies, you know how she likes to roll down them damn stairs and bump her 'ol head.*

The thing is, you've already succeeded as a writer if you are writing. If you're getting paid regularly, you've nailed it (sorry for the Britishisms). If you self-publish books and people read them, you're winning. If you're sitting between myself and Stephen King at a convention, congratulations, you're in with the big boys (obviously joking. King doesn't do cons anymore).

I can honestly say that there is nothing else I would rather be doing than creating, writing, thinking, worldbuilding, plotting, and putting work out into the world for a living.

Well, I can't go back to welding, now, can I?

Writing Questions. Writing Answers
By
Gage Greenwood

As a child, I had two major influences in my life: my mother, and my siblings. My mom was a poet. She had a few published collections of her work, but never really found much of an audience outside of one poem that sort of blew up. To this day, I still run across that poem, etched into a piece of wood, written in fancy calligraphy on a clock, or scrolling down a tasseled bookmark in some random store. No, I won't disclose what that poem is, but I'll bet you've seen it, too.

It's kind of weird my mom tried her hand at poetry. She liked it well enough, but when it came to reading, she was all about the supermarket mysteries and the two big K's of horror (King and Koontz).

While she clacked away on her typewriter in her makeshift office in our basement, I would sit on the floor, playing with my toys and eyeing the built-in shelves behind her, shelves loaded with books. I was a kid, so my poison was Hardy Boys books and Choose Your Own Adventures, but I liked the look of her books, the cool covers, and ominous blurbs.

Which brings me to my other influences, my older brother and sister. The first book I read outside of those kid books was my sister's Edgar Allen Poe collection. I devoured it front to back. Meanwhile, my brother introduced me to all the beautiful and horrific horror movies my young eyes were never meant to see.

I fell in love with horror. Well, I loved it, but I was also a complete baby about it. When I watched Poltergeist, I tossed my Ronald McDonald doll in the trash. No way was that asshole staying around. But still, I loved the genre. I loved that it made me scared enough to pitch my favorite doll.

While other kids were reading short chapter books or foregoing reading at all, I was flipping the pages on Dragon Tears by Koontz, Pet Sematary by King, and Creature by John Saul.

It didn't take long before I put pen to paper and started churning out my own stories. I mostly wrote Tales from the Crypt rip-offs, stories where bad guys got their comeuppance in ghastly and ghoulish ways.

Meanwhile, my mother gave up on poetry, the industry too difficult, time consuming, and a strain on her already complicated mental health issues. Her last hurrah was to try her hand at a children's book, which she diligently wrote before placing it a box, never to be seen again in her lifetime. That book represents the final nail in the coffin of her writing dreams, a series of yellowed papers stuffed amongst old report cards and other junk In the attic.

My mother and I shared something else, too. Mental health problems. For her, it meant extended stays in hospitals where they tried to cure her depression and anxiety. For me, it meant pushing more and more away from normality, not quite understanding something was wrong with me, something that could have been helped with a proper diagnosis. I didn't know OCD was such an isolating and complex mental illness. I just thought it was for people who liked to clean too much. Lord knows, I was a cluttered mess, so it couldn't have been what I had, right?

Watching my mother's struggles made the idea of publishing an outlandish thing for me, and I didn't bother to try, even when I got older and my writing, stronger. Instead, I went as far into the "normal" life as I could. Retail management, engagement, new car, so close to the white picket fence. Then, I lost all of it at once. The company closed, couldn't finish paying off the car I had totaled, and I split with my then fiancée just six months before the wedding.

On top of that, my mother got cancer.

It was around then I decided I was going to pursue whatever the fuck pipe dream I had, no concern for how much I might suck at it, or how difficult it would be, or if I'd end up homeless. Life sucked and death sucked harder, so why waste another minute worried about filling some idealistic lifestyle when I could be happier pursuing the things I loved.

First up... Nope, not writing horror. I became a stand-up comedian.

For about five years, I spent day and night in bars and clubs telling jokes to strangers, something that would eventually help me with my writing. When you have a crowd of eyes on you attached to a bunch of people who want to laugh, you better learn quickly how to get to the punch. Cut out the fat and hit the high notes.

About two years into doing stand-up, my mom lost her battle with cancer, and I lost my will to care about life. I dove headfirst into alcoholism and drugs, discovering it quieted my OCD tendencies, depression, and anxiety. A walking, talking comedian cliché.

And just like most drug and alcohol stories, it ended with me crashing face first into rock bottom about fifteen times before finally cleaning up. I quit standup, couldn't possibly spend a night in a bar during those early days of sobriety. Not that I had much of a standup career left after all the bridges I had burned. Turns out drunkenly yelling at audience members is not a way to advance your stature in the scene.

A few months into my sobriety, I put pen to paper and wrote two short stories. One was called Through Flickering Lights, a Silhouette. The story is about a young girl hunting for her adopted brother in a thickening winter storm. This all happens in a post-apocalyptic setting where monsters called "Lampposts" roam the night. I wrote it because I was trying to picture my grief, addiction, and mental illness from the perspective of someone on the outside. The lampposts represented my destructive personality when I grieved for my mother. The main character was based on my real sister.

The other short story I wrote after finding out the lead singer for my favorite band turned out to be a really horrible human. I had listened to his lyrics after my mom died, during my addiction, and during my early days of recovery. What did it say about me that I so closely related to the lyrics of a monster? So, I wrote a story about a terrible girl who grows up to admire someone even worse. These two horrible people bring out the worst in each other, and their lives intertwine in the worst ways possible. That story is called "Grackles on the Feeder," and remains to this day my most controversial work.

The industry was in a weird place at that time. Quite a few self-published authors had made a big name for themselves, ebooks were exploding, and foregoing the trade route became more common. Still, in the horror genre, the typical path for most authors seemed to be: get some short stories published, then push your book to small pubs.

So that's what I tried, and it worked... Sort of. Grackles on the Feeder found a home in an anthology with some big names, and my first novel, In the Eyes, in the Shadows found a small publisher. Everything was falling into place. Until, in the same week, the guy making the anthology decided he couldn't do it, and the small publisher shut their doors for good.

I was back to square one, but it was a very different square from the one I started with, because we found out my girlfriend was pregnant with our first child. I put the dream of publishing to the side and took a good job with a local company that I ended up becoming the vice president of.

During my time working there, I spent so much mental and physical energy on the job that I hardly ever wrote and missed out on a lot of my son's growing up in his first few years.

When the pandemic hit, I didn't immediately jump back into writing. I was too eager to spend every second with my son while I had the opportunity. But eventually, I looked him in the eyes and said, "He's either gonna have a dad who said he wanted to do things, or a dad who did them."

Shortly after that, I published Grackles and Through Flickering Lights. I also started serializing a story called Winter's Myths. It was weird dystopian, horror, adventure, fantasy... thing. Surprisingly, people loved it. Like everything else I wrote, there was a lot of me in it. After all, it was the story of a family who looked and appeared just like everyone else, but they also couldn't quite fit in, couldn't make sense of the world around them, and spent most of their time frustrated with things most people take for granted. They are walking talking mental illnesses. Of course, there's also Kevin Bacon the demigod, Abraham Lincoln the Ice Giant, and a murderous raccoon named Rapture, because I am not out to drill my woes into my books. I want people to read my stories for the sake of enjoyment, and I want to write my stories to help me heal. I don't see any reason I can't do both. Not everything has to be a treacherous monologue with heavy handed messaging.

If you want to find something deeper in my stories, you can, but you don't need to. There's no overarching lesson to learn in the words. For me, it's just therapy. That's not to say it has replaced professional therapy. I still need that, and it helps immensely, but writing is a way for me to explore myself from an outside perspective, and I need that, too. I'm answering questions I need solved.

I think there's some confusion over the concept, "Write what you know." That doesn't mean your characters need to be plumbers because you're a plumber. It means bring out the big questions, make bold statements, infiltrate your own mind, explore yourself. Write what you know by using your own experiences and feelings to mold a new world. But what might be even more important: write what you don't know. What are you trying to learn about yourself? What can you gain from this story?

Every single story I have written started with a question:

Through Flickering Lights, a Silhouette: What did my addiction look like to those who loved me?

Grackles on the Feeder: What happens when someone idolizes a person that turns out to be a monster?

Winter's Myths: What kind of stories would people create if they saw modern human life for the first time without having someone to explain it for them?

Two Shows on Saturday: Will my past catch up to me and what will it look like when it does?

Bunker Dogs: Can inherited mental illness have pros despite its many cons?

Of course, none of these stories are ABOUT those things. I'm not writing after school specials. You won't read the blurb and see, "a story about mental illness." In fact, you wouldn't even know it's there if you weren't looking for it. That part of the story is for me. The hard work, characters, plotting, editing, formatting, that's for the readers.

I always write with my reader in mind. Some people say they could never do that, but for me, I want to connect with my reader, and publishing is that bridge to connect us. I want the bond that comes from the teamwork. I write, they read. It's a collaboration, and I have them in mind during the whole process.

Writing for them doesn't negate writing for me. It all blows together into a maelstrom of words. We all win in the end. Meanwhile, that first novel I *almost* published, In the Eyes, in the Shadows? Well, just like the children's book my mother wrote, it's sitting there collecting dust. Unlike my mother's last book, it wasn't the end of something for me, but just the start.

No matter how hard it gets, never drive in that final nail. Write for you. Write for them. But keep fucking writing.

Double-edged
by
Christina Bergling

When I was eight years old, my fourth grade teacher stood in front of the class and told us we would be publishing our own books. I was already writing stories all the time, but the idea of bound pages and a dust jacket thrilled me. Years later, at my high school reunion, my former classmates told me they remembered me writing all the time and knew I would publish a book one day.

And I did in 2014.

Writing was always easy for me. The stories amassed in my brain and poured out of me. I was not, however, prepared for the actual business part of being an author. There were so many small details and odd experiences that I never expected.

When I was coloring my homemade dust jacket in class (garishly purple with something that was supposed to resemble a dog), I imagined drafting manuscript after manuscript and sending them off to a publisher. Then I was done. I would be a New York Times Bestseller and onto the next book.

No. Laughable really. I wish I could pat naïve little me on the head.

I never really thought about the finite process. The entire workflow from typing "THE END" to other people reading my published pages was an enigma to me. I didn't think I needed to care about those details. That's what publishers were for, right? Yet now I know that mysterious cloud is full of unforgiving rocks and sharp points.

To be fair, the publishing industry has changed massively since I was daydreaming in elementary school. Not to age myself, but it is unrecognizable from those days. The advent of self-publishing thrust a double-edged sword through the industry.

On the one side, publication became accessible to all. Publishing houses are no longer the cultural gatekeepers. With enough work, anyone can find their way to the page.

On the other side, publication became accessible to all. The market is utterly saturated with no quality standards. I don't need every other work listed on Amazon (or wherever) to come from Random House, but a certain level of proficiency would be nice.

That accessibility definitely contributed to getting my work out there though. I have published through small indie publishers for my five books and 20 shorts. Who knows if any of them would be out in the world if they had to go through the rigors of agents and monopolist publishing houses?

These days, it is in the hands of the readers to find and like what they want. Only the other side of that blade cuts deep. How do they find you in this sea of options? In my experience, they likely don't. Your book may be on Amazon, but it needs 50 reviews with confirmed purchases to be visible. You can promote on social media, but your posts will likely be suppressed unless you pay for advertising. Or pay an influencer. Or pay a reviewer. Or pay a blogger.

I could probably sell more books if I spent more money than I would make.

As an author, it is hard (impossible, even) to break against the tide. With my first book, my publisher provided a marketing and promotion class. The end goal was to enable authors to get our books out there and sold by ourselves.

Did I mention publishers don't push your book now? It's even in the contract that you are expected to do the legwork. How many socials do you have? Your follower count may help you get signed.

Back with book #1 (Savages), after this marketing class, I spent a lot of time on social, connecting with readers and promoting my book. I met all sorts of people, made online friends, and found readers.

Enter the algorithms.

Steadily, my friends and followers seemed to disappear from my feed. I could look them up, but I never saw anything they posted. The connections grew stale, and the fruit they bore shriveled. Likewise, they could not see me. View counts, comments, shares all plummeted.

Unless, you know, I wanted to pay for engagement.

I didn't think it would cost so much to be published. I dreamed I would be drowning in royalties and movie deals. Instead, every year, Turbo Tax rudely suggests I should give up being an author due to how much money it costs me.

I also didn't expect it to cost so much time. When I was scratching down my little stories as a child, I thought being an author was about writing. Only writing and more writing. No one told me I would spend more time prostituting my work to readers online than creating it. I could have written more novels in the time I spent on Facebook and Twitter pushing people to read me.

But wait! There's more... time suck. Even before publication and promotion, the business shoves a cold hand into the process to steal focus. Once the novel is written, editing begins. Editing is a special circle of writer hell. Unavoidable and soul-crushing.

I live in my stories as I write them. I get lost in the worlds (part of the appeal). Yet turning on them to scrutinize and clean them was a black hole of a whole lot I didn't want to do. All the classes with rough drafts and peer edits and "final" drafts did not prepare for me for overhauling a full-length novel. It felt like I was holding puddles of scenes in each hand, trying to reshape them into something coherent.

And once I thought (foolishly and very incorrectly) that the novel was polished and perfect and ready, it moved to outside readers for its beating. Critiques that felt like watching someone kick my baby. The book went to beta readers and editors.

I love beta readers. I adore feedback, even the pointed kind. But beta readers are hard to come by (unless you pay them). There are only so many favors you can extort out of even the most supportive friends and family. The most successful method of harvesting betas I've used is to exchange the activity with other authors or join a critique group.

Beta readers give you an audience perspective. Editors tear your book apart. For its own good, of course.

Outside the publishing house, editors do cost, as any service should. I once paid a couple thousand dollars just to be told to start over. I have had many different editors for each publisher and anthology. Some were better than others, but all were pleasant to work with. It took the solitary exercise of writing and briefly made it a group sport. The collaboration fostered my confidence in the work. Someone else read it and found it worthy (even if they were paid to read it).

That confidence lasted until the reviews started coming in. I have read this advice from multiple famous authors, and I cannot repeat it enough. DO NOT READ THE REVIEWS.

Oh, the reviews. They are the best and worst part of being published. Double-edged again! A positive review was an instant shot of pure joy and serotonin to my brain. They made me feel seen, understood, worthy. They bolstered my confidence and commitment to the craft. It was a high, seriously.

But the negatives ones lacerated my artistic soul. Even knowing that no book will please everyone and that negative reviewers tend to be more vicious does nothing to ease the slice. One negative review easily eradicated ten positive ones. Even a negative review with grammar mistakes. Even a negative review that didn't even address the book. They still made me question my abilities. Briefly at best.

The high is high, but the low is low. I listened to the negative more (like we all do). They made me doubt and question myself. They erased my confidence and self-worth. The price is too steep.

Don't read the reviews. Keep your work pure and get your feedback from the sources I mentioned (and complained about) earlier. Where it's constructive rather than potential trolling.

This is the price of having it all on full public display.

I always knew writing was sharing a part of myself. That was most of the appeal. It was my outlet; I needed to release the dark things inside me. However, I did not appreciate the vulnerability of being fully published. Especially if you tend to rip from your own life and person like I do.

People always assume stories mean something about the author. Like they are some sneaky window into the creator's deep, dark secrets. Sometimes, they are. Many times, the story is just the story. Each artistic choice is regarded as a glimpse into their mind, a measure of their character. I knew this since my writing sent me to the counseling center my entire school career. I couldn't write dark and horrific things if I was not disturbed and in need of help.

Publication just amplified the lens. I cracked my chest open and my heart was on display to anyone and everyone. And I write the dark, twisted shit.

Once again, two blades. On the one side, the audience got bigger. The questions came from friends and strangers alike now. Why do you write horror? Did this really happen to you? Are you really into this? What's it like in your head? What's wrong with you? Show us on the doll where the horror movies hurt you.

On the other side, the audience got bigger. For any negative reviews or awkward questions, there was also connection and fans. I have written about mental illness, and many people have told me that my work spoke to them and helped them. That is worth all the precarious exposure.

That is the point of writing to me, to put out work that resonates with people.

And also because I have to get it out of me.

So it will keep coming out. Even if there is no profit. Even if I still need a soulless day job. This is passion, not profession.

Yet. A girl can still dream. And work her ass off.

Despite the time and money it costs, I'll never quit writing or getting my work out into the world. Since I learned how to scribble on a page, writing has always been a part of my life. I think it will continue to be until my mind unravels. Being published was always in my dreams, always in my plans. It was my primary career goal.

And I made it. It is hard (even for this writer) to describe the euphoria of holding my first book in my hands.

It may not look like I expected. Parts are challenging, some even unpleasant. But it is all worth it. If I could give any advice, I would say keep the expectations low and the motivation high. And don't read the fucking reviews.

We Are Not Alone
By
Jay Bower

Writing horror fiction is a blast. I get to delve into dark subjects, have fun with them, and then safely leave the shadows. But it does come with a price.

Everyday I deal with crippling self doubt. It's a common problem, especially amongst independently published authors. Not having gatekeepers is wonderful, but it also induces a nagging feeling that I'm not worthy. That I'm a fraud. That I don't belong.

Every piece of fiction I let escape into the world is both a euphoric high and a soul-crushing low. I craft stories that I hope my readers will love, but I don't know until they actually read them. Then when it goes beyond my close circle of fans, I dread the reaction because *I'm not worthy. I'm not good enough.*

I know most indie authors, regardless of genre, tend to have a similar experience. I do think mine goes back to two awful encounters I had early on in my career.

Several years ago, I wrote a post-apocalyptic story that had some brutal moments: Parents offering their kids up for sex to rebuild the population. Cannibalism. A ruthless despot who seizes control of the remaining government. It was my first attempt at writing an entire novel in first person and I thought the story was a lot of fun. I finished the draft, revised it, had a couple author friends read it, then sent it to an editor that I was friends with. She was an author like me, but had a growing editing business. Anticipating some red ink but knowing she had my best interests in mind, I sent it off, eager to get the edits back and move forward with the project.

About a month later, I received an email from the editor with the manuscript. Here are some of the comments:

Okay, before you open the file, you need to read the notes here and maybe take a day to think about them.

This was the opening sentence to the email. I clenched. This was gonna be bad.

There isn't anything in this that hasn't been done literally hundreds of times before, and several dozen of those are by big-name authors with some serious talent.

The implication being...I'm not any good. I lacked the talent to dare attempt this story.

There are a lot of other things that seem sloppy or just plain daft.

There are different ways to convey that something isn't working. This wasn't constructive, it was belittling.

This is a form of Deus-ex-machina, and it is the sleaziest trick a writer can pull.

So...I'm sleazy? Again, there are better ways to get the same point across.

I read the email a few times and didn't know what to do. I'd written at least two other novels by this point, but no one had ever slammed me like that. Maybe I fooled myself into thinking I knew how to write? In my mind, she was the "expert," not me. Her comments carried serious weight.

As if this wasn't bad enough, two days after receiving this email, I went to a writer's conference.

One of the activities they planned was a blind slushpile exercise. Anyone that wanted to could drop off five copies of a three page sample of their manuscript. They would select three of them at random, read them aloud, and then the five person panel of small-time agents and small press owners were to raise their hands the moment they'd move on to the next manuscript. They would all then critique it in front of a hundred authors. No one knew who the authors of the piece were and it was completely anonymous. Of course I dropped in copies of this particular story. I believed in it and surely my editor had missed the mark.

The panel read two manuscripts, one of them making it through to the point where they would have asked for more if this were real. Then they got to the third one.

They read the name of the story out loud and my heart pounded in my chest. It was mine. They started reading. Once they all turned to the second page, hands flew up so fast! I just sat there, alone, sipping my soda, wishing I could crawl under the table. They then proceeded to shred it, claiming it was like a movie and how that's not the way to write a book. They hated everything about it and did not hold back with their critiques. To be fair, a couple points they brought up were solid and made sense. I appreciated those. The rest? Brutal.

I was devastated. In the matter of a few days, I went from thinking I was on the verge of something awesome to soul-shattering doubt.

I had an hour-long drive home on a desolate rural highway. I turned the music off and just...thought. I questioned if I should give it all up. Who cared about what I was writing? Who would read it? Apparently I was trash. Everyone seemed to be telling me the same thing. I was a fraud for even trying. I made plans to hang it all up. Clearly I was delusional about my ability.

When I got home, I shared all of it with my wife. She took a moment, then replied. She asked if writing made me happy. It did. Then she suggested I forget the project and try something different and write it for me, write it for my enjoyment and no one else.

It took me a couple of months before I attempted to write anything. I had lost the will. Eventually I broke out my computer and started typing something new, relegating that story to the abyss.

Since then, every piece of fiction I send out to the world has been an exercise in overcoming doubt. Approaching other authors for feedback and – hell, a blurb – is excruciating. But yet, I do it.

I do it because the experience from years ago taught me that my books are not for everyone. Those that crushed me with that book had a solid traditional publishing mindset, which is ok if that's what you want to do. I was, and am, an independent author. I enjoy releasing books on my own and also working with smaller, independent horror presses. I was not part of that traditional publishing world.

Even though they exist, I've learned to push through my doubts and just go for it. Sometimes it works, sometimes it doesn't. I'm ok with that. I'm building something and every good structure takes time.

I believe in myself more now than ever. My readers have instilled that in me. Their support and encouragement means everything to me. It still doesn't chase away the doubt that lingers. If I'm not careful, it will drag me down. I always have to be on guard against it.

Sharing all of this is not meant to discourage anyone from writing and sending it out to the world. I share this to let you know, you are not alone. We all have fears and doubts. We all have a story within us and we are the only ones who can tell it like we do. Your voice is unique and needs to be heard. Go for it. I promise you, someone wants to read it.

Oh, the manuscript in question? It's the only novel I've ever written that has not been published. Most likely it will stay that way. Despite my growth as an author, some things are better left dead.

Bleed Through the Microphone
By
Patrick R. McDonough

I'd like to talk about my journey with the show I created, hoping it might help aspiring podcasters. When I started Dead Headspace in early 2020, I thought it was only going to be a solo endeavor. During that time, I also ran a review platform called Dead Head Reviews. I recruited a small team of reviewers, and Brennan LaFaro was one of them. I asked him if he'd like to record an episode with me and he said yes. We focused on a discussion of Jack Ketchum's *The Girl Next Door*. The chemistry was there from the jump. Everything about us felt right.

It felt *natural*.

So, I asked if he'd like to be a part of the show, and he fortunately said yes.

Since then, I can honestly say, I don't know how I would've gotten through every single one of my bad times in life without him by my side. There isn't another person in the world I would want to enjoy all the good times with, through both of our writing and podcasting careers.

We're always thinking of ways to improve the show, no matter how minute a change it may be and hell, sometimes listeners may not even notice some of the fine-tuning. We chisel away until that block of granite forms into just the right angle or curve. We hone our skills to deliver the most impactful and meaningful show we can offer. Our goal throughout this entire time is simple and clear. A mantra we won't ever change: to document this epoch of writers, primarily in horror/crime/and dark fiction, spotlight every walk of life we can, amplify voices that may otherwise not have the opportunity to do so, and to spread love, hope, and entertainment. We also hope that we're the reason our guests sell a few extra books!

One phrase I think about often as a writer is to "bleed on the page." When applied to fiction, it's a term that means being vulnerable—lowering your shield—and allowing your painful life experiences to flow into your story. That doesn't mean you need to include the real-life names, places, or specific events. Rather, that you're allowing yourself to use those raw emotions as the driving force to add meaning behind the clacking of keys.

Bleeding on the page can expand to other art forms, such as podcasting. Art expresses the depths of human creative skill and imagination, and podcasting can explore that in any and every way possible. There are many ways to achieve that, but I find bleeding through the microphone to be the most rewarding. More on that soon.

There's a lot to consider before recording your first episode, such as, what kind of content do you plan to present? Where do I go for my logo and what do I want it to say to my target audience? Do I make a website? Hire an editor? Hire a marketing specialist? How do I choose a good podcast directory to host my show? Or, one of the biggest considerations, the very framework of your show, will it be scripted, such as *The Industrial Revolutions?* A show that is painstakingly researched, scripted, edited and produced.

Then, there's the unscripted show like *Written in Red*, where they talk to authors and discuss their books and their writing processes. Unscripted is the direction I opted to go in for Dead Headspace, a show hosted by Brennan LaFaro and myself. Dead Headspace is a conversational show that focuses on getting to know the person or people behind the art. More times than not, we go in a direction we didn't see coming.

Brennan and I started Dead Headspace as an audio only show. It was fun, but it wasn't until the eleventh episode that we tried recording with video as well. Throughout the first season, recording in video was dependent on guest requests and special circumstances. It wasn't until our second season that we fully committed to bringing video *and* audio to our viewers/listeners. The reason we've continued recording in video is due to how intimate and personal it is. It's the next best thing to a face-to-face conversation. You can read the other speaker's body language, which helps indicate when you can jump into the conversation. When you look at each other, you can often feel what they feel, and that's where bleeding through the microphone takes effect.

When you're comfortable with someone, it reduces the stress of anxiety. That stress-free environment is what Brennan and I strive for and pride ourselves in creating. A place where people can feel safe and truly be themselves. We've had some really special heart-to-heart moments where we get personal and emotional, and yes, tears were shed, both in laughter and sadness for the stories that were shared.

When you bleed through the microphone, there's a moment of catharsis. It doesn't happen during every conversation, that's not a realistic expectation, but it does always happen organically.

In those moments, everyone is swept away by the speaker's shared emotion. It's truly a beautiful thing.

Dead Headspace has grown into something bigger than I ever imagined it would become. If you asked me a few years ago if we'd record over 200 episodes (that's over 400 hours, that's just about 17 days STRAIGHT of listen-time), I'd shake my head and say you're out of your mind. We've been lucky to do what we do, and even luckier to have been able to help many people in so many spectacular ways.

If you want to start a podcast, you absolutely should. Since beginning Dead Headspace, I've been granted the opportunity to talk to authors I've admired for years. It has also opened doors for other areas in my career, and best of all, has allowed me to grow strong friendships, some being familial.

For those that take the dive into the podcasting world, I'll leave you with some advice that I was given early in my career from two writers I greatly respect. The further you progress in your career, the uglier some people will act toward you. Never forget who you are and the quality of your heart. Don't allow strangers to lower your self-worth. Keep your eye on the prize. Don't forget why you started your show and focus on the things and people that make you happy.

Always be your genuine self *especially* in the face of adversity. Never stop pursuing your dreams, make happiness and peace of mind your goal in life, and surround yourself with good people. Try to remember that every single one of us—yes, even the person you may dislike most in life—has more in common with you than you may like to admit.

But ... you'll never find any of this out until you have a conversation. A *genuine* conversation.

To achieve all of this, I say to you, bleed through the microphone.

Shaping a Legacy
By
Joe Mynhardt

What do you dream to achieve in your lifetime?

By the time you finish this entry, I want you to take a few minutes to think about your goals.

It's nice to dream, right? Which of course means *nothing* without action, and that's what I want to discuss with you. I will share parts of my publishing journey, what I'm doing to ensure my legacy, how I'll be remembered once I'm gone, and how to create a strong foundation and sturdy steps on the way up the ladder.

WHERE IT ALL BEGAN...

All great journeys need to start with passion. For me that passion is stories, whether it's a book, short story, movie, or even a game. I've always wanted to write, but at the root of that was the desire to create something out of nothing. So once I wrote and published some of my own short stories (I had just over 60 stories published in magazines and anthologies between 2008 and 2012), I quickly realized that I enjoyed the business side of publishing much more than the writing. I've always had a knack for business, which I believe I got from my dad.

But I was still a fan first. Especially short stories. I believe it was 2011 when I reached out to some authors just to say well done (more on that in a bit). I read their stories and just wanted to say how much they touched me and to thank them. For me, I get the same chill on my skin that a great song will give most people, so when a magical story comes along, I can't help but be moved. The only author who's managed that constantly is of course Stephen King. His short stories can be phenomenal. John Connolly is another favorite

In 2012, I decided to put together an anthology. Since I live in South Africa, I had to register with the IRS for a tax identification number, and for that I needed a company name. What's better than Crystal Lake when it comes to a horror fan, right? Since it's not a name that fits exclusively to the horror genre, it gives us the opportunity of genre expansion down the line.

I invited some authors I'd met online after reading their work, or sharing anthology line-ups with, and the rest is history. Crystal Lake Publishing launched in August 2012 and we released that anthology around March of 2013. I went on to publish short story collections by quite a few of those authors, and eventually their novels.

I take pride in the fact that I worked hard and was my true self with those authors. I became great friends with a lot of them, and went on to promote their careers like I was their agent.

As the company grew and became more established, one contact turned into five and so on, because authors talk to each other. They recommend publishers and editors and tell you who to avoid. Do a great job and be a good person, and word will spread. Reliability and trust is key. You'll be invited into the fold and you'll end up inviting others into that fold. Good, caring, and kind people love working with likeminded folks. I don't care how talented you are or how much money you can make me. If you're an insufferable fool, well, then you're sealing your fate. You can't even hide that from readers these days.

THE PUBLISHING BUSINESS:

What is it like being in the publishing business?

Honestly, it can be an absolute dream or a nightmare. Hopefully you'll land somewhere in the middle and work your way up, but that takes time and patience.

Being in the horror community is definitely like being part of a very special tribe or community.

There are lots of them out there, but not many are this special.

But...every territory comes with predators and somewhat unstable characters. You'll have to choose how active you want to be and accept the consequences.

My advice is to be as active and involved as you're comfortable with. Protect yourself. Be in control of your surroundings, your brand, and your future. Part of that means also double checking your contracts and *using* contracts for everything you're involved in. Whether you're a publisher, editor, author, or artist... If someone challenge you, don't even reply emotionally. Just quote the contract. So... Protect! Your! Self!

Also, don't compete. Unless it's a bit of friendly competition that brings out the best in you.

Don't be jealous. If others succeed it just shows you that it is indeed possible. Support them and learn from their success. Share in each other's successes. Be an example of success. We're not envious and really do help our fellow publishers.

The magic behind Crystal Lake Publishing is that even though we've grown from a small press to a medium sized press, we keep in touch with our roots and continue to function as a small press. Not ignoring authors or only focusing on our bestsellers.

We treat our authors well, giving each the same amount of care and attention. This means that even if we're working on six or more book launches at the same time, no author feels slighted or that we don't care.

It's hard, but part of this business is putting on quite a few different hats every day and trying to focus on the small details while working on the bigger picture. If it wasn't for my comprehensive to do list, I'd definitely swap things around accidentally because of all the different book launches we're scheduling and building up to.

Use social media, not just for marketing and branding, but to help you see what works with other presses/authors, and of course what went wrong with some. Dissect their problems, learn from their mistakes, and put safeguards in place for your company or brand. Yes, even if you're an author, you are the product and the brand. This is a business/career, after all. Even if you are an author going after the traditional publishing route, study self-published authors. We live in a time where even a big publisher can't promote you effectively if you're not going to take part in the process.

With any business, there's a lot of politics going on. Try not to be pulled into the drama, but always know what's going on. I try to, but constantly find myself on the outside. I just don't have the time to read Facebook/Twitter posts and follow hashtags. But I have some author and publisher friends who keep me in the loop. I do also subscribe to the most important publishing newsletters.

PERSONAL STORIES

I have way too many personal stories to share with you at this time. But a few highlights do come to mind. For instance, publishing some of my favorite authors for the first time. Names like Graham Masterton, Neil Gaiman, and Jonathan Maberry come to mind. Personally interviewing Wes Craven a few months before he passed away. Also Jack Ketchum. Sending emails to and fro with Clive Barker. Holy crap, right? Had some great email exchanges with Mick Garris. I really hope I never get used to these exchanges.

Over the years I've been there for many friends during life struggles. Lots of battles with cancer. And they were there for me when my dad and sister passed away only a few months apart.

A great author friend arranged to meet up while he was touring South Africa with his family. We're actually making plans to meet up again next year. I'd drive for days to see them and I'd do it for a lot of the amazing folks I've met over the years. Probably better that I'm not living in the States. I'd always be on the road, traveling to every convention or book launch.

ADVICE

- Be reliable, nice, caring, and kind. You have no idea how far this can take you. But please, don't even try to fake it. So let's add *be sincere*.
- Follow the guidelines when you submit a story or even contact a reviewer. If you don't have time to read the guidelines, why should editors/publishers invest time in reading your work.
- You are only limited by your own knowledge and creativity, and of course by time; not by how many hours you have (we all have the same), but by what you do with them. How you balance those hours between work, self-improvement, and mental and physical wellbeing. How many hours you spend in creative thought and actually putting those thoughts into action. It's so easy to be busy for an entire day without getting much done. I also have those days. We all do. Remember these words: We overestimate how much we think we can get done in a day, but we underestimate how

much we can get done in a year. Crystal Lake grows in leaps and bounds over the course of a year. And I hope I do, too.

• Set goals. Lots of them. Give yourself realistic timelines and break those goals down into smaller goals and steps. Have an action plan. And then act! Too many people only see the end picture and then just sit and wait for it to magically happen.

• Do what needs to be done while keeping an eye on your wellbeing. This is a career. Long term is key, and if you burn out, everything you've done will just fade away. If you just keep adding more and more onto your workload, you'll be too busy and start making sacrifices you shouldn't make. Working too hard can quickly become a bad habit, which means you actually feel guilty the moment you're not working. It's not just hard work that leads to success. It takes a balance of so many things. I've had days where I felt like just pushing through. Working easily 18 hours straight. But the next day my mind would just be foggy. I didn't sleep well. I was tired. And yes, even my body felt the burden. On those days I hardly got anything done. Wouldn't it have been better to just stick to nine hours a day?

I would've felt better, perhaps worked faster and thereby getting more done. I would've had more time in each of those two days to make sure I still kept everything balanced, spending enough time with family and perhaps a friend. Distracting myself with a hobby or even a movie. I'm sure a lot of you know some extremely hardworking people who never got a break in life or achieved success. Balance is key! For how much work and things I've accomplished, and how much I can get done in a week, you wouldn't know it, but I still find to watch movies on an almost daily basis. I even play games. I spend a lot of time with my four-year-old daughter, who I raised while working from home. As I mentioned earlier, movies and games (and yes, books) feed my soul, because I love stories. It requires a lot of planning and organizing, and it also means *getting stuff done* when it's time to work. I never spend more than five minutes a day just surfing the web, and I focus on one project or issue at a time, doing what needs to be done so I don't get overwhelmed.

   • Putting in the work does not always mean doing more, but doing less of what doesn't work. Working hard and smart.

Which of course comes with experience. I always say stick with what you have time for and what you're comfortable with, and if you have to stop doing something, remember that you can always pick it up again later. The world is constantly changing, and so should we.

- There's nothing wrong with taking a day or so off. Learn to listen to your body and mind. Having a goal or even a self-applied deadline should not put unnecessary pressure on you. Remember, you're doing this because you love it. Nurture that love.

- I didn't mention spending time with friends because that's one part I neglected in my thirties. I didn't nurture my relationships and didn't have the time to make new ones. Back then I worked two jobs. I was a teacher by day and publisher by night. I decided I wanted to pursue this publishing career as a full-time job and sacrificed whatever I could to get here. Mission accomplished, but I definitely could've found the time to nurture friendships. So please, learn from my mistakes.

- Also learn from the mistakes of other publishers and authors. As a publisher, there are certain golden rules. Don't use your authors' money, for instance. Plan and budget. Never risk it all in one move. No possible setback should ever be able to sink your company.

- Becoming successful requires strategy and planned approaches. Networking. Yes, who you know does make a difference. Remember when I said I reached out to authors after reading their stories? It was sincere at the time, but I realized later that it was a brilliant business move, as well. Today I have working relationships with most of those authors. We need each other in this business, and we're mutually beneficial to each other. So, who you know does make a difference, and it's not at all unfair. We all did the work, put in the time. We all put ourselves out there and were approachable and kind. We're all of similar minds and became good friends. We all share the passion and love for this business, and we're kind and reliable, so why not work together whenever the opportunity arises.

- Be open to those changes and new challenges. Be prepared for the opportunities. Prepared for the success to come. Expect great things *every day*. In this business, an email can change your life. Keep building a great reputation and great people will be drawn to you. Opportunities will come, but also keep an eye out for them. Grab at them. Be creative. Then, create opportunities for others.

- I've experienced so many highs in my career that I quickly became used to them. Used to the excitement and the rush, but sometimes you go through these long stretches of business as usual. The same is true for an author. But I eventually realized that I can get that same rush and excitement from helping others. It's that same feeling of watching your loved ones opening gifts you got for them.

- As an author, look for a press with a solid foundation. Be careful of those who are hot right off the bat. It's possible, but they tend to burn out quickly. They might not exactly know what they're doing right. Once they hit a snag they don't know how to handle it and will most likely be unable to recuperate because they don't have a strong foundation to fall back on. I'm proud to say that if I make a mistake or find myself in a situation where someone is throwing mud at me or the company, I'm in the position to just ignore it, because authors and fans and folks in the industry know enough about me to know that I'm solid guy. That this person is not speaking the truth. I remain professional and show my integrity. This only comes with years in the business.

• Plan and work like you'll live a hundred years. Plan with a sense of urgency like you only have one year left. Love what you do or find something else. Have a passion for it and the people you surround yourself with. Care about what you provide. Quality above quantity. But don't let fear of bad quality keep you from delivering. You can only edit that first draft so many times, right? I, for instance, love motivational quotes and videos, because they remind me of my goals. Why I'm doing this and what I set out to do. What I want my future to look like. They make me reflect on my goals and motivate me. Like an established author helping out a new author, we also learn through teaching others because it reminds of us where we came from. It also reminds us of the fundamentals that we probably forgot. It's part of what we do and it's infused in us, which is great, but we need those fundamentals to remind us of our love and passion for the written word. It helps show us how far we've come.

Well that's my time. Thank you for reading. If you don't know it yet, do know that I'm looking forward to meeting you, perhaps even working with you. Helping you. Yes, you.

Now go out and pay it forward! Your legacy lies not in physical things, but in the knowledge and memories you instill in those left behind.

My legacy will grow from living and teaching the words I just shared with you. Perhaps more, right? I'm always open to new things.

How will we remember you?

Write from the Heart
By
Sarah E. England

The best tip on writing, in any genre, I ever had was from a magazine editor I used to write serials for. It was to show not tell. This way the reader is involved in the story, feels what the protagonist is experiencing and thus becomes more engrossed and their enjoyment increases. It means the reader is not held at arm's length and feeling the story second hand.

Consider the difference:

1. Lucy threw herself on the bed feeling very unhappy with how Max spoke to her. He'd annoyed her intensely and she felt like crying.

2. Lucy threw herself on the bed. Rage erupted from deep inside her, hot tears stinging her eyes. How dare Max speak to her like that! Who the hell did he think he was?

I had always wanted to be a writer but as a teen I wasn't given much of a choice regarding what to do for a living, and had to leave home. I was forty before I got the chance to study the craft. Although, English literature was a passion and the one subject apart from art that I'd been any good at, I did have to learn how to write fiction and it took a while. My first short stories subbed to magazines were all returned. Looking back now I can't believe I sent them in! The best advice I can give is not to take rejection personally but to use it as a growing tool... those critiques, providing they're constructive, are gold. I will always remember the first time I had an acceptance. After that they rolled in, and all together I had 160 short stories and serials published before attempting a novel.

Ultimately, with a desire to write about the supernatural, it became more difficult to 'write to order' in genres that held less interest, so I became an indie. Publishers didn't want occult horror and supernatural thrillers. It would have been about 8 years ago now that I hooked up online with some talented writers and artists, editors and digital formatters, and set off on a journey of, 'let's see what I can do.' It's been very challenging and I don't make much money. But I'm not in it for that. I want to create and somehow I get through. I'd say – learn the craft, learn the marketing, help each other, and connect with your readers. Also, what do you want to say? What is the message? The core, driving force, or heart for doing what you do? For me, synchronicity came in the form of someone who told me a story – someone who formed the basis for Ruby in Father of Lies. It felt right and it came from

the heart. After that, people who read it wanted more.
I hope that helps someone.. just believe in yourself.

Writing to Market
By
Ash Ericmore

Write to market. That was what they said. That was what they *still* say. And that's right, isn't it? Romance is popular. Write that. Fantasy is popular. Write that. The US market is huge, write for that.

I call shenanigans.

And it only took me twelve years and almost quitting writing to work that out.

You see, the thing is, I tried. I tried really fucking hard. I wrote a series of paranormal fantasy books. They were good. They really were. And they were to market, but can you imagine my foul mouth filling the mouths of YA fantasy witches? Christ. It sold *so* well (read: none). I wrote short stories for publishers, and heck, I even got some of them accepted. In US English, set in the US (having, at the time, never even been there). I wrote thrillers, because they were popular. I wrote lashings of fantasy. I wrote *clean* with no swearing or anything. I wrote to satisfy those people who I didn't know, writing material I didn't know, in genres I didn't read—or sometimes particularly like—because I was *writing to market*.

That's not what anyone should take away from *writing to market*, and so to a certain extent, don't go writing to market at all.

It's sort of like the *write what you know* conundrum. I mean, I write a lot about psychos and serial killers. I'm neither (*laughs nervously*). But it's write what you know, not *what* you know. Clear? So yeah, after that twelve years of following every piece of sales and marketing advice that landed on my mat, and failing to sell anything at all, I changed *everything*. I changed me. I changed what I wrote, and who I wrote for.

And you know what? I outsold twelve years of books in three months, with one novella.

Write to market.

If you want to write a series about a sentient armchair that eats people, then you know what … you can. Just do it *to market*. I hate to tell you, but there's already someone that's written something like that. But that's okay. It doesn't matter. But what does matter is that, that means there's a market already. That is the market you're writing to. Not some hoity-toity pony riding set who buy a lot of romance books. No. It's the salt of the earth weirdos who only read psychotic armchair fiction. That's *your* market. And if you want to write that, that more than likely means that you already read it. So *you* are *your* market. And that means you know your market.

So you need to write for you, for that market. You need covers that are to market. *That* market.

And it's so easy to look at writing advice like that and jump on to write what's popular. But it doesn't work. You have to put yourself in your writing (*writing what you know, duh*), and if you're not writing for something you have some intense passion for then it wouldn't feel right to the reader … and they won't like it. You know, like if some loser Star Trek fan tries to write an awesome Star Wars book, it'll just suck right?

The audience will know if you're being disingenuous. And they'll tell you they know with their wallet.

Write what *you* know. Write what *you* like.

Don't write to market. Write for you.

Rest if You Must, But Don't You Quit
by
R.E. Sargent

Being in the indie horror community has been an interesting ride. If you had asked me ten years ago if I ever thought horror would become popular again, like it was in the eighties, I would have come back with a resounding "NO." And if you had told me that not only was horror going to explode again, but the indie horror scene was going to also, I would have pacified you and possibly said, "Well, bless your heart!" But now, just look around you. The indie horror scene is huge, and some of the authors in the community are giving the big names a run for their money. Book contracts are being signed, people are buying T-shirts and merchandise representing their favorite books and authors, and bookstores such as Barnes & Noble are bolstering their horror sections to the point where the indie horror books outnumber the traditionally published authors. Even Stephen King should take notice that his tomes are not the only occupants of the horror section now.

Being part of the scene is exhilarating. The passion and support that the readers show are like no other. They, as a group, are loyal, dedicated, and just plain awesome. This is evident by the ever-growing TBR piles stacking up in their homes.

Being a horror author is a rollercoaster of emotions. On a good writing day, everything seems to click. Other days, it's pure torture trying to get the words on the page. Finishing a project takes you up, and then getting a crappy review can take you down, if you let it. Many people suggest that you don't look at reviews. They can be a motivation killer. But, if you have to look, be prepared...no matter how good your book is, there is bound to be someone who won't like it...and that one person who thought it was the biggest piece of shit ever written. Yeah, that guy. He is most likely a troll, or another author that is jealous. Whatever the case, it's important not to let those harsh words derail you. Come out swinging harder. Look carefully at what was said and analyze if there is anything you can improve on. Is there a smidgeon of any truth to anything he said? If so, use that to fuel your writing fire. And also, fuck that guy. He doesn't matter.

I really enjoy being an author, and because I appreciate books in general, and also well-done anthologies, a few years back, I decided I wanted to try my hand at publishing. One of the anthology series that really inspired me was the Hot Blood series. I reached out to my good friend and fellow author Steven Pajak and pitched an idea for a series to him, and he wanted in immediately. Little did we know that out of that idea, an indie publishing company would be born. What is even more amazing to us is that it is doing great and is well-received. Why do I mention this? Because many authors get the urge to dip their big toe in the publishing pool. In fact, I have seen many of my writer colleagues open up their own publishing houses. That urge may hit you as well, if it hasn't already. If it does, I'd like to offer my unsolicited advice should you decide to go for it.

Firstly, be cautious of what you schedule for publication and make sure your life will mesh with that schedule. Many of us have full-time jobs and families in addition to our writing careers. Adding a publishing business to the mix can be taxing, especially when you do multiple publications each year. Something usually will need to give in order to create extra time for the process. Usually, that sacrifice is either writing, reading, family time, or sleep. In my case, it's all four. Start out slowly and build momentum as time permits.

Secondly, make sure you have a decent budget set aside for each publication. Publishing takes money, and cutting corners will not only produce an inferior product, but it will affect your reputation as a publisher. Budget for story payments (and make sure you are following the average out there), editing, quality covers, interior formatting, advertising, and did I mention editing? Yes, I mentioned it twice, because no matter how good you are, you also need at least one more pair of eyes on it.

And third, have fun with it. If it ever becomes a chore, or if it consumes all your free time and stresses you out, consider slowing down a little. If it robs you of the time you need to do things you are passionate about, think twice about it. And I mentioned dipping your big toe in the pool earlier...think about doing that to start, instead of jumping in headfirst, unless you have lots of time and resources.

Anyway, enough about publishing. There is more to talk about on the author front. There is an important word of advice I have for all of the new and aspiring authors out there. It's so important that you choose a name to write under that you will love forever. If that's your real name, then you are all set. If you decide to choose a pen name, choose wisely, and take some time with your decision. I can't count the number of people that have told me they wished they had chosen something different, but it was too late, because they had already gained a following under the name they were using. A name can always be changed, but you run the risk of starting over. It's better to get it right out of the gate. I can relate to this... I too regret the name I chose to publish under as I am noticing the publishing world is saturated with authors using their initials, and to me, the names just don't resonate as much with the readers as a full first and last name. That's only my opinion, but it's something to consider.

One other thing I noticed early on in my writing career is that there are people that will love you and embrace you and others that will see your success and try to destroy you. When I published my first book, it got a lot of attention, and unfortunately, it attracted the attention of a troll, who I later found out was a failed author that could not get published. He proceeded to talk shit about me and ridicule me in every online forum he could, going so far as to leave a one-star review for my book, which he never read. This went on for months until I was able to successfully not only block him on all avenues, but get him kicked out of the groups he was harassing me in. Eventually, I dropped off his radar, but a couple years later, I saw a few people post about the same guy, who was doing similar things to them.

As a young writer, this situation almost destroyed me. Many authors have imposter syndrome at times, myself included, and when this happened, my self-doubt was on ten, and I almost quit writing. In fact, I stopped writing for a good six months, until I decided I was not going to let him win. I'm glad I didn't, because I love where I am at as an author, and I am gaining steam every day.

When it comes to being an author, my best recommendation is to find your tribe. Find those that support you and have your back, and surround yourself with them. Stay away from the people and groups that are negative or cause you angst. Don't be afraid to leave a Facebook group or to block someone. For me, the best thing I could have done for building relations with readers and other authors is join the *Books of Horror* Facebook group. Most of the people there are amazing, and I have made so many great friends and gained so many readers and fans from there.

One of the things I struggled with, when I was a new author, was self-doubt. I thought my first novel was pretty good, and the plot was well-received. But reviews were mixed, and people either loved it or hated it. The common theme for the negative reviews was that the dialogue was stilted and some of the scenes were unrealistic. It took me awhile to realize they were right. Sometimes, our pride gets in the way and we dismiss those comments, citing the reviewer as crazy, but one thing I learned is feedback is a gift, and even though a negative review can hurt our feelings, we need to analyze the comments and determine if there is anything we can extract from them to make ourselves better at our craft. I won't pretend my feelers didn't get hurt along the way, and I certainly have had some extremely brutal feedback over the years. I even had one editor beat me up so badly that I discontinued using them, not because of the content of the feedback, but because of the delivery.

But the bottom line is that when I was closed off to the negative comments, I wasn't growing, but when I got past the hurt and really looked at the information being given to me (and mind you, this feedback is free), I was able to adjust my writing patterns and get better with each piece I wrote.

That leads me to another point. Very few writers are great out of the gate. I have seen only a handful of debut authors that have a mega-successful first publication, and when it happens, it is magic. For the majority of us, we release something that is okay, and then we improve with everything we write. Don't set unrealistic expectations for yourself…you will only wind up being disappointed. Many newer authors get discouraged and frustrated. Negative feedback or sparse sales discourage them. My advice on this is to think of a writing career as a marathon, not a sprint. It takes many years to build a budding writing career. And it also takes drive. A backlist is also helpful. One or two published works in your back catalog usually won't get you to where you want to be. Set yourself a writing schedule and stick to it, even when you aren't feeling it. Get the words down on the page. It doesn't matter if they are good, only that they are there. You can fix them later. And, when one piece is complete, jump into the next one immediately. Publishing regularly is important to keep your work fresh with the readers.

So how did I get started on this rollercoaster ride of writing and publishing? Let's just say I have always been a bookworm since I was little. When others were outside playing sports, I was inside reading a book. I have always been passionate about reading, and around 1991, I picked up a used book in a bookstore by Dean Koontz. The title was *Night Chills*, and to be honest, I had never heard of Mr. Koontz before. I was so hooked on the book that I had to read more by him, and so I bought another, and then another. That passion for his books led me to start collecting them, and I am now the proud owner of one of the most complete Dean Koontz collections in the United States.

Over the years, I met Mr. Koontz many times at book signings and even bumped into him once in a bookstore in California that he wasn't doing a signing at. My early exposure to his work sent pulsar messages to my brain that said, "I want to do this...I want to be a writer!" And so I became one. I decided I wanted to write a novel right off the bat, and I wrote it, on an electric typewriter no less. It took me well over a year to finish it, but I finally did. And then, I tried to get it published and found that to be extremely difficult, as out of all the hundreds of queries I sent out, I was only able to contract with one agent, who ended up scamming me. (This is the part where I tell you that no legitimate agency or publisher should be charging you. If they ask for money up front, run.)

This was a time when the only type of indie publishing that existed were vanity presses where you actually paid to have your book published, and you typically had to buy a bunch of copies and then try to sell them. I wasn't interested in that route, so I gave up. (This is where the title of the story comes in.)

How long did I give up for? Twenty years. Yes, you read that right. Over the course of those twenty years, I occasionally tried to renew my efforts, sending out a stack or two of query letters to agents, to be met with no interest. My attempts at rekindling my efforts sputtered out quickly each time I tried, and I felt it was never going to happen for me. Then one day, I stumbled across a product online that I wanted to buy, and I realized that it was something called "Print on Demand." I thought that was a great idea: the customer places an order for something and then the company makes it and ships it out. My brain began to work overtime, and I thought it would be great if there was a company that could do that with books. So I researched it and was dismayed (and excited) to find that the technology had been around for years and I never knew.

Regardless, a fire was immediately lit under my ass, and I knew what I had to do. I immediately took the time to do an extremely heavy edit/rewrite on my first novel, I hired an editor and a cover designer, I found a company that did book interiors, and I self-published. It was so amazing to see the immediate finished product. After I published the first one, I immediately moved into the second novel, and then the third. An entire new world had opened up for me, and I was no longer restricted to being at the "no" end of an agent's pen.

It wasn't until after my third novel that I started writing short stories, which is backward from what most authors do. I saw an open call for submissions, answered it, and wasn't selected, but that just fueled my fire more. Eventually, we started our publishing business, and many of my stories were included in our anthologies. I also started getting invites to other anthologies as well, which is a great feeling.

This leads me to my next bit of advice. The internet is a powerful thing. Use it to your advantage. Join as many writing Facebook groups as possible. Join groups where publishers post open calls. Familiarize yourself with where to find the most information, and frequently check for calls that fit your writing preferences. And then write and submit. And don't worry if your work isn't accepted for an open call. It happens to even the most seasoned writers. Just keep pushing, keep moving. But one word of caution: publishers write specific submission guidelines for a reason. They want what they want and how they want it. If you feel the guidelines don't apply to you, or you disregard them, because *maybe they will make an exception in your case*, you are just going to leave a bad taste in that publisher's mouth. So do what they ask, submit, write, and repeat. And, if a story continually gets rejected, try to get feedback from people you trust on what the story may be lacking. We are too close to our own work to always be objective, so getting outsider opinions and suggestions is paramount.

So, let's talk about the word "indie" for a minute, which, of course, is short for "independent." According to the Alliance of Independent Authors, "An indie author is a writer of fiction, nonfiction, or poetry books who self-publishes their own work and retains and controls their own publishing rights." Others may call indie authors "self-published." While there has been some stigma attached to self-published authors in the past, especially by some authors that believe that traditionally published authors are the only "real" authors, I am happy to say that I personally see less and less of that bias each day that passes, and there seems to be a wide acceptance of indie authors, to the point that some supporters prefer indie books over traditionally published, due to the quality of the writing as well as the personal interactions they can typically have with an indie author. Most indie authors will chat with you online and even send you signed copies of their book. Any they are oh so grateful for your support. You are not just a number to them. So, for those readers that support indie authors, and especially indie horror, I salute you. You know who you are!

So, if you are a writer, keep on writing no matter what. Don't let life derail you…go after your dreams. And remember, the only one who can get in your way…is YOU!

These Hybrid Moments
By
Robert Essig

There was a time when self-publishing was not only frowned upon, but shunned. It was laughable. A sure sign that some failed author couldn't accept the reality that they weren't good enough, so they went ahead and published their magnum opus on their own, or, god forbid, they chose a vanity press. That is a term that still causes my flesh to crawl. I can hear faintly the shrieking of violins from the shower scene in *Psycho*. Mere leeches, those vanity publishers, wicked vultures preying on eager writers who don't know any better.

But things have changed as far as self-publishing goes. Things have changed drastically over the past ten years or so. The stigma is vanishing, or at least it's lessening, the foul taste not more accepted, but accompanied by better fruit. The pool of self-publishing is still rife with the detritus of shitty cover art, no editing, and bad writing. But there are some serious gems out there. There are authors who are making a living by self-publishing. There are great works of fiction coming down the self-publishing pipeline.

But is self-publishing for all of us? Of course not. I actually think there's a better method out there, and that's called being a hybrid. What is a hybrid? Quite simply, it's an author who is both traditionally published and self-published. I see many advantages to this, and I see many authors out there using this method.

I know that when I started out, the idea of self-publishing was loathsome. This was around the time that it was starting to be accepted, but still had a heavy stink surrounding the concept as a whole. The old heads balked at young authors who were dipping their toes into this pool. I saw it play out on social media many times, just like certain folks hold onto the double space after punctuation for some goddamn reason. It's an easy habit to break. Believe me. I for one needed the confidence that came from a publisher willing to put time and money behind my book. Did I make mistakes? Hell yes. But I have learned from those mistakes, and they would have been worse had I dove into that murky pool of self-publishing without knowing a damn thing about how publishing works. Even when publishers screwed me around, I learned from the experience. I built my name. I put myself out there as much as I could. I worked with many publishers and have found out which ones are class acts and which ones can fuck off, and I still make mistakes. Even the good ones can fuck up. We've all been screwed at least once. If you haven't, are you even trying? I also learned how publishing works. The nuts and bolts of it all. Industry stuff that is not nearly as interesting as writing the stories, but necessary if you want to successfully publish your own work.

After years of small press publishers, I realized that I wanted control over at least a few of my books, that way no matter what happened, I could depend on those titles being there, being available. I could stock up on copies for events without having to send emails and wait for a response. I could better track my sales. I could offer promotions, discounts, etc., whenever I wanted. I could give away however many copies for review I so desired without any kind of backlash or uncertainty from the publisher. Sounds pretty great, right?

Yes, but how many of us have the kind of extra money that affords things like cover art and editing? Not I. And I certainly hope you're not reading this thinking you can do the cover and editing yourself. Maybe the cover. But don't you dare edit the book yourself. I won't get into the nuts and bolts of what goes into self-publishing, but know that money goes into it. Set a budget. Understand what you can afford to lose, because your first books will likely not make a damn thing.

That brings me to the whole hybrid method that I'm so fond of. I write a lot of books. Mostly novellas and short novels. I like putting out two books a year published through small presses. As of writing this I have a book out with D&T Publishing, and another coming out later this year from Encyclopocalypse Publishing. Setting those releases apart like that gives me room for my self-published stuff that I release through my Infected Voices imprint. I prefer to publish novels with my small press publishers and release novellas in between. There are several reasons for this, but mostly it comes down to cost. Novellas cost me a lot less to publish. With less words, the editing is cheaper (and note that editors like when the books are as clean as possible). Cover art? Do your research. There are cover artists out there offering great work at budget prices. I know some people are rolling their eyes, but it's true. Don't settle for less. Just be vigilant and you can save money and still have a quality product. You might even have a knack for cover art. That's cool too, but don't fool yourself. Maybe ask some trusted friends for their opinions. As for formatting, I bought a program called Atticus that has everything laid out and is really easy to use. There are plenty of people out there who offer formatting services, but that will cost you.

You can't expect your publisher to do much when it comes to promoting your book. Most of them don't do much at all. Do your research. Work with publishers who give a damn. Once you understand the self-publishing game it might seem like you don't need traditional small press publishers, but if you choose the right ones to work with (assuming they, in turn, choose your work to publish), then you have access to their fan base. That's one of the most important parts about this hybrid method. A quality product that you don't have to pay for doesn't mean jack if no one is buying it. If the publisher is established and has a following, that's a pool of readers who will potentially read your book merely for having been published with said small press. And if they like your book, they will buy more of your titles.

Keep in mind that most contracts are for about five years. Hold onto the edited version of the manuscript. File it away on your computer and back it up on a thumb drive. Hell, save the email for future reference. Once that contract is void, or earlier if you request your rights back, you can acquire new cover art and re-release the book under your own imprint. Breathe new life into it. The rights to my book *Stronger Than Hate* were just released to me and that's exactly what I'm doing. Being that the book had already been edited, and I still have the edited Word file, all I have to do is purchase cover art and format it. The book had a good run, but it's been stagnant for a while now. Under my own imprint I will make it thrive once again. That right there is the hybrid method working for me.

Your release schedule is very important. If you dump your books in a cluster all at once, you can't expect them to compete with one another and find success. I made this mistake one year and saw certain titles flounder while others did well. That's like chumming the waters and hoping the readers grab something. You have to work with your publishers and let them know your schedule. Don't assume they know what the fuck you're doing. They don't. Most publishers are flexible if you discuss release dates early in the publishing process. I find it's better to get my traditional publishers squared away before I decide when I'm releasing my self-published books.

The idea behind being a good hybrid is that your books are helping one another sell. Your efforts are divided between yourself and your publishers so you're not doing all the heavy lifting, and also so you're not in the dark. Asking a publisher about your sales figures is expected, but infrequently (unless you want to piss them off—remember, they work with many authors). If you want to track your numbers daily, you can do that with your self-published stuff. This will give you an idea of what promotions are working, or anything you might have changed in your social media presence or your newsletter that might have garnered sales. You can apply those changes to the promotion you do for your traditionally published titles. That's information you wouldn't be getting were you solely a traditionally published author.

Lastly, always feel free to ask questions. It might seem like surrendering your manuscript to a publisher and having them deal with it is the easiest thing to do, that all the nuts and bolts of self-publishing are too difficult to understand. Reach out to writers you've communicated with on social media who are veterans of self-publishing. You'll find that many of them are quite responsive and eager to share what they've learned. Relinquishing your manuscript to a publisher is like handing over control to something you've spent a lot of time cultivating. A hybrid author retains some of that control, and I feel that makes traditional publishing that much easier to handle, because no matter what happens to a publisher who has your hard work under contract, you will always have control over enough of your assets to manage while correcting course.

Advice From Steve
By
Steve Stred

When Kevin J. Kennedy contacted me about potentially submitting something to this anthology, I wasn't sure if I'd come up with something, but I also had no idea how to go about doing it. Usually, you have your submission guidelines! So, I hope this works for those reading it!

After thinking more about the prospect of sharing some advice, I knew I needed to submit something – I'd be way back at the starting line still if others hadn't shared advice with me when I was starting out.

First – write for you. Write the stories you would want to write. If you're not enjoying what you write, readers won't enjoy what they read.

Second – don't chase what's popular. Readers will know when something is formulaic and lacks feeling. It doesn't matter if it's Romance, Sci-Fi or Splatterpunk, a book with an emotional pull will always be more enjoyable than something devoid of feelings.

Third – find an editor you gel with and forge a relationship. An editor is there to make your work better, whether you want to hear it or not. Take their criticism constructively – that's what it is.

Fourth – take pride in your book cover. People DO judge a book by its cover. Find a brilliant cover designer and have your cover pop.

Fifth – DO NOT engage with bad reviews. Reviews can help you become a better writer and can point out things you need to work on, but reviews are for readers – ignore bad reviews and move on.

Sixth – encourage, support, and lift up your fellow writers. You are not in competition with anyone else but yourself. I always say – we need more we and less I. A like, share/retweet, comment etc goes a long way.

Seventh – celebrate all your victories. Finishing a draft, getting cover art, receiving an acceptance, acquiring a blurb and of course when your work releases into the world – celebrate them all! You've accomplished something and should be very proud.

Eighth – celebrate other author's victories. They've accomplished something and it's a wonderful moment.

Ninth – never concern yourself with sales or what you expect or predict. There is A LOT of amazing work being released all the time. Releasing a book and having it take off is like catching magic in a bottle. Stay the course. Work on your craft, release solid, engaging, strong books and cultivate a fan base.

Tenth – lastly, you'll always been your own worst critic.

To anyone reading this and thinking about writing something but you're not sure if you can – YOU CAN and YOU WILL. DO IT. I believe in you. Now, believe in yourself.

Steve Stred is the 2X Splatterpunk-nominated author of 'Mastodon', 'Churn the Soil,' and many, many more. He lives in Edmonton, Alberta, Canada with his wife, son and their dog, Cocoa.

He is an active member of the HWA.

So, I wrote a book, now what?
By
Candace Nola

The world of indie publishing is not an easy one to navigate, full of authors all doing the same thing, trying to be seen and heard, tiny rowboats in an ocean full of steamers and cruise ships, hoping not to succumb to the undertow or be eaten by the Great White sharks of the business.

How then, do we compete with Blake Crouch, Iain Rob Wright, Jonathan Maberry, Bentley Little, Matt Shaw, Victor LaValle, Paul Tremblay, Joe Hill, or... *gasp,* the King? **We work**. Period. Day and night. Put in the work. Pay your dues. Grind and grind harder. And accept that it's not a competition, not at all, even though it can feel like it.

Readers, real readers, read thousands of books in their lifetime, and there are millions of readers in the world. There is room for us all. The key is to get those readers to notice you, without the backing of traditional publishing, agents, and publicists. In my recent journey down this path of indie publishing, I have learned many things from so many great people that I cannot begin to thank them all. What I can do, however, is pay it forward, which has been my motto since day one, and something that I carry out every single day.

That being said, what do you do now? You have a finished manuscript right there in front of you, waiting for your next step. Do you know your next step? Did you do your homework? Choosing to go indie means you are the one making all the decisions. You will need to choose an editor. You will need to decide on using an indie publisher or will you self-publish? What about a cover? Can you afford a cover artist, or will you design your own? Interior formatting, distribution platforms, trim size, matte or glossy, paperback or hardcover, I could go on. All these things are important but before any of that, almost even before you write the first word, there is one thing I want you to think about first. Branding.

Who are you? What does your current social media presence say about you right now, if one were to do a search? Would a reader follow you based on your current posts, tweets, or behaviors? Would an employer hire you based on what they might find? The moment an author decides to publicly state they are an author, they become a public figure and their life is no longer as private as it once was.

While many people will not agree with this mindset when first reading it, I implore you to realize that it is true. As an author, you are providing a product to customers, books to readers. The exact same concept as a manufacturer providing food, car parts, clothing and any other millions of items that people consume daily. As the creator of the story, the author is now their brand. **You** are your brand, your representation of what the reader is buying.

What reason are you giving them to purchase your books? Why should they choose to support you when they can choose from hundreds of others? Sure, they may enjoy your books, but would they enjoy your political views, or those distasteful memes, or hurtful, harmful, or careless remarks on various posts online? Being in this industry as long as I have now, going on six years, I have seen hundreds of readers drop an author due to their behavior online, their posts, their attitude, and many other reasons.

Yes, the author is still a person. You can still have a life, opinions, and views but if you also want to be a public figure with a wide fan base, you will need to think about how you are representing yourself to your readers. There is a way to speak intelligently about your views without being volatile, disruptive, arrogant, harmful, or rude to your readers or to those that are of a different opinion.

The moment your book comes out, the moment you announce you are an author, everything changes. Readers will look at your media, personal posts and more, to determine if you are worthy of their money. You are no longer Joe Smith from Wyoming but author Joe Smith of BIG NEW BOOK.

This idea applies to everything regarding your life as an author in all public spaces, written or recorded, on all social media sites and even your reviews on distribution platforms. How you choose to engage with your readers will be observed and studied. Bad behavior will be talked about, posts will be made, and readers will stay away. Likewise, fellow authors will stay away.

A new author will get nowhere without support from other authors. How do you get that support and keep it? The same way you gain that support from your readers. Learn the etiquette of the industry. Learn how to approach other authors, what the protocol is for sharing promotions, requesting blurbs, or asking for feedback or mentoring. Learn how to use the various groups on social media that are there to help you navigate the business. Go in willing to learn, not demanding help. No one wants to help anyone that comes across aggressive, arrogant, or entitled.

Almost ninety percent of the indie authors that I know all have day jobs. They spend every moment of their spare time writing, marketing, editing, promoting, and helping others. Be respectful of the time they choose to invest in you. Be appreciative and do your part to pay it forward. Not a single person that has helped me has asked for anything in return, but I do what I can to help others, any way that I can. Believe it or not, all of this also goes into building your brand. You are not just creating a brand for the readers to believe in, but your brand builds your reputation for other authors and publishers too. A good brand is easier to get behind, simple fact.

If this seems ludicrous at first, that's fair. It's not easy to realize that we give up most of our personal lives to do what we love so much, but this is the reality of it. Ask yourself what would you do if the author you admire so much was suddenly revealed to stand for everything that you go against? That they support things you loathe or engage in harmful behavior against others that you simply cannot ignore? Would you still give them your money, or would you find someone more worthy?

It's simple, really. Treat others as you would want to be treated. Be kind. Be supportive. Engage in useful intelligent discussion. Offer and be open to honest feedback. Be worthy of the readers' faith and trust in you, and that of your peers, and by doing so, you will build that fanbase and author network that you want, one person at a time.

10 Steps to Becoming an Author
By
Mark Lukens

1. READ A LOT – WRITE A LOT

The best, most succinct, advice I've ever heard about writing comes from Stephen King and his book *On Writing*: Read a lot, write a lot. Before you ever entertain the idea of becoming a writer, I believe you should have a love of the written word, a love of writing, of creating new worlds and characters. Yes, I think writing should almost be a compulsion for you, something you *must* do. I started writing short stories when I was eight years old. I was inspired by sci-fi paperbacks pulled from my parents' bookshelves (and of course, everything I wrote at that time was a cheap imitation of Ray Bradbury). Even though I had fallen in love with writing, I didn't ditch books. I read even more. I read different authors, different genres. When I was fourteen years old, I read my first Stephen King book—Christine. "This is what I want to write," I told myself. And even after that epiphany, I read other genres and authors. I read classic literature as I got older, I read everything I could get my hands on. Even before I stumbled across Stephen King's simplified equation of writing advice, I was already reading a lot and writing a lot. The hours have to be put in; I'm not so sure there's any way around it. Are there writers with natural talent? Of course. But do those writers still have to practice and keep those writing muscles strong? Of course. So, before you even start your first draft or your first short stories, keep reading everything you can get your hands on. And keep writing. And finish what you start, even if you don't like it at first. You just might find new ideas popping up as you write, as the curtain magically draws back from the mind's eye.

2. WRITE TO MARKET OR FOLLOW YOUR PASSION

Do you want to make a living as an author, or are there stories you feel compelled to write? There's nothing wrong with either (or, ideally, a combination of both). Everyone's idea of success is different, and it can be everchanging. Some may measure their success by how many books they sell, or how much money they make, or the engagement from readers. If it's more about money, you may want to study the markets and write to those markets. There are many books on that subject, so I won't delve into it too much here. But if you're going to write to a certain market, like a niche in science fiction or romance, then you'll need to read a lot in that genre. You'll need to know it inside and out. Readers will be able to tell if you're faking it. But there's nothing wrong with following your passion either. And you may just have that one story you need to tell, a story that's been building inside of you for years or decades. There's nothing wrong with that either. You can always define your own success.

3. INDEPENDENT OR PUBLISHER

Once you decide to write that novel (or even a series), are you going to want to try to get with a publisher or go independent? If you go with a publisher, you'll need to decide between a large publisher or a smaller publisher. Most likely you'll need to get an agent if you want to be published by one of the major publishers (or their imprints). You may not need an agent for mid-list publishers or smaller ones. Research agents online and learn how to write a brief, professional query. Only send them what they request, and wait to hear back from them. If you're going to go independent, then all you need to do is write the novel and then follow the instructions about uploading the manuscript onto Amazon, or whatever other platform you'll be using. There are also hybrids—authors who both self-publish and have other books with publishers. There are pros and cons for all these choices. Yes, the barrier to entry is much easier as an independent author, but you'll have to do much more of the work and marketing yourself. There are plenty of success stories for all these choices, you'll just have to select the one that best suits your needs.

4. IDEAS – WHERE DO THEY COME FROM?

Where do you get your ideas? That may be the most frequent question to an author. My answer: I'm not really sure. Ideas just seem to pop up sometimes. Usually, they're not fully formed, just a faint glimmer of an idea that may or may not turn into a story or a novel. If an idea's really intriguing to me, I like to jot it down on paper. I may or may not do something with it later. It may become its own story, or it may feature as part of another story. If ideas don't come easily to you, then you can hash out ideas with your family or friends. You can read news stories or articles online that may spark an idea. Reading books and watching movies or TV may spark other ideas. Remember to write them down, because sometimes even great ideas can be forgotten or become muddled later on. If you like an idea, draw it out further on paper. To me, there's some kind of magic at work when pen is put to paper, that curtain of the mind's eye drawing back again, new ideas forming as fast as I write, the deeper into the story I explore. I can get ideas while on the edge of sleep, or while mowing the lawn, or driving to the store, or watching a show on TV. I would advise keeping a small notebook in your car, or even on you, for when those little nuggets pop into your mind.

5. OUTLINE OR PANTS IT

There seems to be two camps when it comes to this subject: some write outlines before they begin their first draft, others start with some vague ideas and just begin writing, seeing where the story takes them (this is sometimes called seat-of-the-pants writing, or just pantsing it). I can't give much advice here, because I'm definitely more of an outliner than a pantser. I've tried pantsing it in the past, but I would just end up writing myself into a corner or having to go back and change so much as the story changed along the way. I've always been pretty detailed with my outlines, breaking the outline down into rough chapters, with a line or two about each one. I like to know where the story is going, how it's going to end, who the main characters are, the major plot twists. I do believe there can be a happy medium between the two. I like to do a rough outline, but it's not chiseled in stone, things will change as the first draft begins (that's what I referred to before as the magic that happens once the writing starts), and I like to go with those changes most of the time. But the choice is up to you—do what feels more comfortable to you; if it gets you writing that first draft, it's going to be helpful. You could try both of them and see which one works better for you, or (like I do) a hybrid of the two.

6. THE FIRST DRAFT – THE VOMIT DRAFT

I heard the first draft referred to as "the vomit draft" because you vomit everything into that first draft. No one writes a perfect first draft. You will always have to go back and edit, change things, punch up dialogue, fix typos, reword, add scenes and take some away. You may have to do multiple rounds of editing, especially with your first few books. So, give yourself some freedom with the vomit draft, vomit it all out onto the paper. Try to write it as quickly as you can. Don't worry if it doesn't sound so great to you at first—you can always go back and change things later (that's what editing is for). But you can't edit or make something better that isn't on the page already. So, get that first draft down on paper or on the computer screen. And once the first draft is done, give it a few weeks to "breathe." Go work on the next project that you're outlining if you're working on something new, or the next in a series. If you don't have another book planned just yet, just take a few weeks off to put some space between you and the work. When you come back to read it, you may find it's better than you remembered. And then you can begin the work of editing.

7. MAKE IT BETTER

Editing. As I said before, I've never heard of anyone writing a perfect first draft. It's difficult for me to imagine any artist being perfectly satisfied with their work. I don't often reread my books that are in print because it would be too tempting to go back and tweak the story, to make it better. Maybe that's why it takes me longer to write novels and stories, because I can be a bit of a perfectionist, never truly happy with them, always thinking they could be better. But at some point, you have to let them go and move on to other projects. So, of course you must edit your work (or pay someone to edit it, but you'll still need to polish it as much as you can before handing it off to your editor), you must write multiple drafts and make your story the best it can be. If you've constructed a pretty solid rough outline, you may not have to do many structural changes, but you'll still want to check for typos, check word and phrasing choices, punch up description and dialogue, make the story clearer. If you have beta readers (readers who are willing to read your work and give you feedback), that is an invaluable help. Listen to their feedback. You don't have to always agree with them, but at least consider what they have to say. If you have many beta readers (like more than five) and more than half aren't happy about something in your story, then you may have to consider that they're right about that aspect of the story and that you're wrong. But in the end, you are the author and it's your story—the choices are ultimately up to you.

8. JUDGING A BOOK BY ITS COVER

Once the final draft is done and ready to go, you'll need to design a cover for it if you're an independent author. If you're going with a publisher, they may design a cover for you. If you're designing your own cover there are a few choices you have: you can design one yourself, buy a premade cover, or have a professional cover designer do it for you. Most times, I would advise hiring a professional to design your cover. That doesn't mean that you can't have an idea of what your cover should look like. You should research your niche or genre and try to come up with a cover that is comparable, one that looks like it belongs in that market. Readers *do* judge books by their covers, and sometimes an intriguing cover can stop a reader for a few seconds, enough for them to read the description or the reviews, see if it's a book they want to read. The cover is very important and it's worth it to spend the money on getting the right cover for your book. There are also some great premade covers on various websites. And if you are skilled in art and design, you can create your own cover. My covers are probably 60/40 at this point: Sixty percent from a professional cover designer, and forty percent premade covers with me doing the lettering.

9. GETTING THE WORD OUT

Marketing and sales. You've written your book (or the beginning of a series), you've had a great cover designed, written an intriguing description to draw the reader into buying your book. Now you need to let them know that your book is available. There are many ways to do this. You can buy ads on Amazon, Facebook, and other social media pages. You can build a following through a newsletter or email campaign. You can use a book funnel by giving away a free book to get them to not only sign up to your email list, but also get them interested in reading the rest of the series. You can do newsletter swaps. You can post on Facebook, Instagram, Ticktock, and other sites about your book. You can join book groups on social media pages. You can go to trade shows and conventions. There are many ways to advertise, and there are many books and courses that can teach you how to do this, but however you do it, you really need to get your books in front of readers' eyes.

10. REPEAT THE PROCESS . . . IF YOU WANT TO

Your book is out there, and now it's selling copies. You've been running ads and posting videos, doing whatever you can to get the word out. So, what do you do now? Sit back? Relax? Yes, maybe. If you just wanted to write the one book, then that's it. You've done it. You're now a published author. There are people actually reading your book, reviewing it, contacting you and letting you know what they think of it. But if you want to write more books, or the next books in the series, then you need to get to work right away on it. Yes, you still need to keep marketing your first book, but get started on the next book right away. One of the best ways to keep your ranking higher and get more readers noticing your books, is to get new books out. How often? Every few months is a good target, but at least two a year, if you can. If not, then just do the best you can. We all write at different paces. If you're a slower writer, or more of a perfectionist, it may take you longer to get new books out there. Some authors can get six or eight or even ten books a year published, others are lucky to get one or two. It's not a contest, you just do what helps you in your own idea of success, and what fulfills you and makes you happy.

I hope this helps someone out there.

The Killer Mentality
By
Nick Roberts

Step 1: Read Stephen King's, *On Writing*.

Step 2: If you want my two cents, proceed with caution. What works for me, might not work for you. I've developed my routine through trial and error.

When asked to contribute advice or suggestions to this anthology, that devilish little voice in my head immediately said, "Hell no. You don't have any knowledge worth passing on. You're barely an indie author yourself. You can't even get an agent. You've amassed a small following and sold a few books, but you're not Stephen King. Hell, you're not even Stephen R. King. You're not in bookstores across the country. You're not going to get nominated for any awards; you don't have the name, and the publishing industry is not a meritocracy."

Man, no one can beat myself up like I can.

I had to take a step back and examine myself; specifically, my thought pattern. Through a little cognitive behavioral therapy technique, I observed this negative train of thought for what it was and let it pass. The fact is, I've met very few writers who haven't had to deal with that pessimistic ear gremlin at least once. Yes, after getting that first publishing credit—paid or unpaid—you'll get a little boost of confidence that'll help keep you going. And with each successive credit, the voice of positivity gets a little louder. Sell a few books and then comes imposter syndrome.

This is where the killer mentality must emerge from somewhere within your primal brain. Rising above the doubts, the fears, the *excuses*, is what separates the ones who finish what they start from those who don't. It doesn't matter if you're the most methodical outliner or a fearless pantser, at some point in the writing process, that voice will tell you to quit.

Kill that voice. Excommunicate it from your skull, march it out behind the toolshed, and whack it with a mallet. Just to be sure, grab the axe from the chopping block and bury the blade into its kneecap, only so it doesn't follow you back. Hell, you've come this far; you might as well grab a shovel, carefully place the tip in the nape of its neck, and stomp down with the force of your fiercest keystroke. Go ahead and use the shovel to bury the mess and cover up the crime.

Once you're back inside and settled in front of your preferred writing device (mine is a MacBook Air), write away. Do so with a target word count in mind. When I'm writing a novel, I don't get up until

I've hit at least 1,000 words. Most times I go over, but I rarely exceed 2,000 in one sitting. Keep in mind, I'm married and have a teenager, a six-year-old, and a newborn. My day job is teaching, so that comes with its own unique brand of stressors. The only time (aside from weekends) that I can sneak away to write is at night, and sometimes I have to *make* that time. But I also must be disciplined and efficient enough to hit my count and get enough rest for work. The Word of the Day is BALANCE.

If this was easy, every aspiring author would have a manuscript or story or poetry collection or screenplay...whatever. Bottom line: if you don't put in the extra effort, remember that there are thousands of others doing it right now. Channel your killer mentality before your competition knocks you off.

When I finish my first draft, I send it to four trusted beta readers. These are family and friends, both in the industry and not. Some are horror fans, others not. What I want them to do is catch any glaring plot holes, typos, spelling/grammar mistakes, and to note what worked for them and what could be improved. I give them a deadline, compile all their feedback, and make changes according to my gut. You don't have to take everyone's suggestions.

When I had the manuscript for my first novel, *Anathema*, I submitted what I thought was a well-edited document to a micro publisher. That book was released in 2020, but the lack of professional editing and formatting stood out. That publisher shut down during COVID, and the rights reverted back to me. Rather than see it go out of print, I formed an LLC and re-released it as a second edition under my company, Spooky WV LLC. That's the current version available through me and other book retailers.

I did the same "editing" process when I wrote *The Exorcist's House* and submitted it to Crystal Lake Publishing. They accepted it, and I thought my part was done. Ha! My manuscript went through substantial rounds of editing and revision with professional editors/proofreaders. I learned quickly to develop thick skin and take their suggestions as constructive criticism. (Though it still irks me that one of their comments was "And this is the part where I throw the book in the trash!") The final product turned out better than I expected and succeeded both commercially and critically. So, if there's a tip to take from that, it's to toughen up and realize that people want you to have the best book possible, even if the truth hurts.

With my third novel that has yet to be published as of this writing, *Mean Spirited*, I am querying agents in an attempt to take another step up the literary ladder food chain. Querying agents is an art in itself, and since I don't have an agent yet, I am no expert on how to land one. The rejection letters have shown me how subjective the publishing industry is. Agents want books they can sell. Even if you have a great book, if they don't feel like there's a market for it, they'll pass. Again, thicken your skin.

Now, let's say you have a book that you're ready to take to market, whether that be through self-publishing, small press publishing, or traditional publishing, what do you next? As I once heard Jay-Z say in a Kanye West documentary, "Closed mouths don't get fed." I took this advice to heart when it came to promoting my work. I have no shame in self-promo; I'm proud of my work. I think my stories are good enough that *I'm charging people money to read them*, so why would I feel like a snake oil salesman with a few promo posts on social media?

If you have a product that you believe in, you must spread the word. Create an Excel spreadsheet. Do some research and find horror book podcasts/interview websites/blogs/popular YouTube and TikTok reviewers and reach out to them. If you have a good publisher like Crystal Lake Publishing, they'll plug you into the network of active reviewers. From my experience, most shows/websites are looking for content and will be glad to accommodate you.

Regarding social media, create author pages for all platforms and make them uniform. Your "brand" should be easily identifiable no matter if you're on Facebook or Twitter. Go the extra mile when it comes to posting content. Post reviews of other books, create engaging/funny videos or contests, and NETWORK WITH OTHER AUTHORS. Find authors you like and watch what they do. See what works and what doesn't. Once you have a growing following, devote some time to a newsletter. Some authors use Patreon, but I've never messed with it.

I am aware, as should you be, that everything previously mentioned is a tall order, especially when you need to be writing AND reading (reading *is* writing) on top of it. Like I said earlier: BALANCE. Work hard but remember that writing is a passion, and passions are meant to be enjoyed. Don't look at the white screen with its flashing cursor and feel intimidated. You're creating worlds. You're providing a much-needed distraction. Write the book that you want to read and get it out there to the people.

Step 3: Repeat Steps 1 and 2.

Success?
By
John R. Little

When anybody starts out on a career, particularly in writing, they hope to be successful.

But what does success look like?

For some, success is having a large publisher take you on – a publisher who markets your books around the world. You'd make enough money to live off your writing, and maybe you'd see your name on the *New York Times* Bestseller list.

That's the dream, right? Hell, it was my dream at one point, but of course it never happened.

All my books (23 and counting) were published by small presses or self-published. Does that mean I don't have a way to count my writing career as a success?

Nope. Over the years, I've found many other ways to think, "Hmm . . . that's pretty darned cool."

I'm going to list here some examples from four of my early books, all of which were published with very small companies. I could carry on for a much longer article, but I think there's enough here for you to see why I count my writing career as being a success, albeit not in the same terms I originally thought of.

I hope that when any indie writer looks back, they'll think fondly of many aspects of their writing. Money is nice, but it's not all there is.

So, without further ado . . .

The Memory Tree

The Memory Tree was my first novel, and when it was published, I was terrified. It was a time travel novel partly about a thirteen-year-old boy who was being sexually abused. That part of the story was pretty much autobiographical. I hadn't seen any books like that before, and I was worried everyone would call it trash.

It didn't help that the tiny publisher went out of business a couple of weeks after my book was published.

But the reviews were astonishingly good. People recommended the book all over the place.

And then a surprising thing happened.

I started to get emails from readers who had themselves been sexually abused or whose own children had been abused. These people were full of hurt, regret, and guilt.

The messages kept showing up, and over the years I've received many dozens. They all had a similar message:

> *Your book helped me to realize I'm not alone, and that others had suffered and*

> climbed out of the abyss. And it wasn't my fault.

Or:

> Your book helped me to really understand what my daughter (or son or nephew or sister) has gone through, and it allowed me to reconnect with him/her.

The letters always ended the same way:

> I'm so grateful that you wrote this book.

Talk about feeling humble. These letters came from total strangers, who somehow had their lives affected by something I wrote.

No better definition of success than that.

Miranda

Miranda was my third published book.

Before publication, I reached out to some authors to ask if they would read it and (if they liked it) might provide a blurb for the back cover.

One of those authors was Peter Straub. I had no real expectation that he'd read the book or even bother replying to my email . . . but he did.

Straub was a giant among horror authors, with amazing books like *Ghost Story*, *Julia*, and

Shadowland, stories I loved. I admired him as much as any author.

To my surprise (and even shock), he read *Miranda* and wrote a fairly lengthy blurb that did make it to the back cover of the book. He called the story, "dazzling, melancholy, and thoroughly gripping."

What???

Peter Straub said that about something I wrote??? Hell, Peter Straub *read* something I wrote? I didn't know how to respond without seeming like a snivelling sycophant.

I've gratefully received many blurbs and reviews over the years, but this one was special, and yes, I count this as a big fat chunk of success.

Ursa Major

My ninth book was about a grizzly bear who traps a man and his stepdaughter inside a small storage area inside a deserted cabin. It was really about my relationship with my own stepdaughter, which already made the story very personal (and successful) to me.

Like my other books, this one got good reviews and friendly emails arrived from folks who read it.

How this one was different, though, was one email that showed up out of the blue a couple years after it was published.

> *Hello, John. My name is xxxx, and I'm a producer with xxxx. I read Ursa Major on a flight from London to Los Angeles and I immediately decided I wanted to ask if the screen rights for your book are available.*

Well, then.

I've had feelers for books before but never from a well-known Hollywood producer. We worked out an option and soon after, money started arriving. Over the course of a few years, I received more than $30,000 (U.S. dollars) for just the option on the book. For doing no work at all, since the book was already written.

The producer hired a screenwriter and I've read the screenplay, which I love because it's very close to my original story.

Alas, the special effects available at the time couldn't make the story fly and they had to abandon the project.

End of the story? Nope.

Fast forward to this spring (2023). The same producer contacts me to say she wants to re-option the book, because special effects available are way better than they were a decade ago. More money is arriving, and hopefully this time, the movie will be produced.

We'll see! But count this up as another success in my eyes.

Little by Little

My twelfth book, *Little by Little,* was my second short story collection, and it was nominated for a Bram Stoker Award.

Three of my earlier books had also been nominated . . . the three I've already discussed above (*The Memory Tree*, *Miranda,* and *Ursa Major*).

Miranda won in its year, which was a stunning development for me.

But, really, all four nominations were a high point in my career. It showed that books from the small (tiny) press could be respected and admired by the horror field.

If you're writing in the small press or self-publishing, there no reason for you to think you're not successful.

Your book might be exactly what somebody else needs. One day, it might appeal to somebody famous or to your peers in the horror writing business. It might lead you to other opportunities.

And you may find something totally different – your own definition of success when you look back on your career.

Don't give up.

Afterword

Well, you made it to the end of our little book. I hope you got something from it. While I can't imagine that any one person could use all the information in this book, I hope you picked up something that helps you get where you are going a little quicker. I also hope we have managed to bring you into our world. The Indie publishing world can be full of pitfalls and disappointment, but it can also be the place where dreams are made. Whatever we do in the future, the main goal for all of us is to entertain. It means giving up a little piece of ourselves to indulge in our own madness. We take time away from family and loved ones to spend time creating. It's not always fun, but for some of us, it is a necessity. Whether you read this book just to get to know some of your favourite authors a little better or you are on your own Indie Horror journey, we all wish you success.

Kevin J. Kennedy

Author Biographies

Lee McGeorge
Before stepping into fiction, Lee enjoyed a career in hospitality, working in 10 Downing Street, Buckingham Palace, the British Embassy in Berlin and some of London's most exclusive hotels. Originally from Hartlepool, he now considers North London to be his rightful and spiritual home.
http://www.lee-mcgeorge.co.uk/

I am **Candace Nola**, and I am an award-winning author, editor, and reviewer. I write poetry, horror, dark fantasy, and extreme horror content. My books include Breach, Beyond the Breach, Hank Flynn, Bishop, Earth vs The Lava Spiders and The Unicorn Killer. I have short stories in The Baker's Dozen anthology, Secondhand Creeps, American Cannibal, Just A Girl, The Horror Collection: Lost Edition, and Exactly the Wrong Things with many more coming throughout 2023.

Beyond the Breach, won the "Novel of the Year" and my Debut Novel, Breach, was nominated for "Debut Novel of the Year", for the 2021 Horror Authors Guild awards. I am also the publisher and editor of the 2022 Splatterpunk Award Winning Anthology "Uncomfortably Dark Presents: The Baker's Dozen."

My best-seller to date is Bishop, currently available on Amazon, Barnes & Noble, and many other platforms. The second installment, Bishop: Man vs

Monster, was released in April 2023, and is planned to be a five-part series.

I am the creator of Uncomfortably Dark, which focuses primarily on promoting indie horror authors and small presses with weekly book reviews, interviews, and special features. Uncomfortably Dark Horror stands behind its mission to "bring you the best in horror, one uncomfortably dark page at a time."

I also own and operate 360 Editing, which is an editing service geared toward new and indie authors to provide quality editing at affordable rates.

Find me on Twitter, Instagram, TikTok and Facebook and the website, UncomfortablyDark.com. Sign up for her Patreon for exclusive content, free stories, and more.

Website: www.uncomfortablydark.com

Mercedes M. Yardley is a dark fantasist who wears poisonous flowers in her hair. She is the author of Beautiful Sorrows, Apocalyptic Montessa and Nuclear Lulu: A Tale of Atomic Love, Pretty Little Dead Girls, Darling, and won the Bram Stoker Award for Little Dead Red. She lives and works in Las Vegas. You can find her at
Mercedesmyardley.com

Russell James grew up on Long Island, New York and spent too much time watching late night horror. After flying helicopters with the U.S. Army and a career as a technical writer, he now spins twisted tales best read in daylight, including horror thrillers Dark Inspiration, Q Island, and The Playing Card Killer. He authored the Grant Coleman Adventures series starting with Cavern of the Damned and the Ranger Kathy West series starting with Claws. He resides in sunny Florida. His wife reads his work, rolls her eyes, and says "There is something seriously wrong with you."
https://www.russellrjames.com/
@RRJames14, or say hello at rrj@russellrjames.com

Sarah England is a fiction writer based in the UK. Originally a nurse, she began writing for magazines around 20 years ago, before writing her first novel. At the fore of Sarah's work is the bestselling occult horror trilogy - Father of Lies, Tanners Dell and Magda. This was followed by The Owlmen, a spin-off from the series. Stand-alone novels include, The Soprano, Hidden Company, Monkspike, Baba Lenka, Masquerade, Caduceus, Groom Lake, and The Droll Teller. Each book explores new aspects of the supernatural, with most set in ordinary, if spooky, surroundings. The Witching Hour is a collection of short stories.   Coming next... 'Creech Cross'... A

supernatural thriller expected by August 2023. Why not sign up to Sarah's newsletter so you'll be first to hear about the next book? Updates are on the blog.
https://www.sarahenglandauthor.co.uk

John Everson is a former newspaper reporter and the Bram Stoker Award-winning author of *Covenant* and thirteen other novels of horror and the supernatural including *NightWhere*, a 2012 Bram Stoker Award Finalist. Other titles include *Siren, Violet Eyes, The House By The Cemetery, Voodoo Heart* and his giallo homage *Five Deaths for Seven Songbirds*.
Praised by *Booklist* and *Cemetery Dance; Kirkus Reviews* called his work 'hard to put down', while author Edward Lee said, 'Everson is a MASTER of the hardcore; he's the rare kind of writer who's so good you can't proceed with your day until the book is finished.'
Everson has written licensed stories for *Kolchak: The Night Stalker, The Green Hornet, The Vampire Diaries* and Jonathan Maberry's *V-Wars*. In 2019, *V-Wars* was turned into a Netflix series that included Everson's characters Danika and Mila Dubov. Learn more at www.johneverson.com.
http://www.worldhorrorconvention.com/
www.johneverson.com/books/the-night-mother/

http://www.johneverson.com/books/cage-of-bones-and-other-deadly-obsessions/

Tom Deady's first novel, HAVEN, won the 2016 Bram Stoker Award for Superior Achievement in a First Novel. He has since published several novels, novellas, a short story collection, and the first book in his middle grade horror series. He has a master's degree in English and Creative Writing and is a member of both the Horror Writers Association and the New England Horror Writers Association.
www.tomdeady.com

John Durgin is a proud active HWA member and lifelong horror fan who decided to chase his childhood dream of becoming a horror author. Growing up in New Hampshire, he discovered Stephen King much younger than most probably should have, reading IT before he reached high school—and knew from that moment on he wanted to write horror. He co-founded Livid Comics in late 2020, co-creating and writing his debut comic titled Jol (pronounced Yule), a Christmas horror series for all ages. After publishing that, the itch to expand his writing was one he had to scratch. Through Livid, he wrote his second comic which released in the spring of 2022 titled Dead Ball. His true passion was always to write horror novels, and in 2021 he started submitting short stories in hopes of getting noticed in the horror community and launching a career. He had his first story accepted in the summer of 2021 in the Books of Horror anthology, and an alternate version of the story in the Beach Bodies anthology from DarkLit Press. His debut novel, The Cursed Among Us released June 3, 2022, to stellar reviews. Next up, his sophomore novel titled Inside The Devil's Nest, released through D&T Publishing in January of 2023, followed by his debut collection, Sleeping In The Fire in June of 2023.

Twitter- @jdurgin1084
Website- www.johndurginauthor.com
Instagram- @durginpencildrawings
TikTok- @johndurgin_author

Eric J. Guignard is a writer and anthologist of dark and speculative fiction, operating from the shadowy outskirts of Los Angeles. He's twice won the Bram Stoker Award, won the Shirley Jackson Award, and been a finalist for the World Fantasy Award and International Thriller Writers Award. His latest books are his novella *Last Case at a Baggage Auction* (Harper Day), novel *Doorways to the Deadeye* (JournalStone), and short story collection *That Which Grows Wild* (Cemetery Dance). Visit Eric at: www.ericjguignard.com or Twitter: @ericjguignard.

Joe Mynhardt is a Bram Stoker Award-winning South African publisher, editor, and mentor, as well as the founder and CEO of Crystal Lake Publishing. Since its founding in August, 2012, Joe has published and edited short stories, novellas, interviews and essays by the likes of Neil Gaiman, Clive Barker, Stephen King, Charlaine Harris, Ramsey Campbell, John Connolly, Jack Ketchum, Jonathan Maberry, Christopher Golden, Graham Masterton, Damien Angelica Walters, Adam Nevill, Lisa Morton, Elizabeth Massie, Joe R. Lansdale, Edward Lee, Paul Tremblay, Wes Craven, John Carpenter, George A. Romero, Mick Garris, and hundreds more. Yes, hundreds. Just like Crystal Lake Publishing, which strives to be a platform for launching author careers, Joe believes in reaching out to all authors, new and experienced, and being a beacon of friendship and guidance in the Horror/Dark Fiction fields. In 2017 he started a coalition of small press publishers to support both each other and their authors. Joe also became a work-from-home dad in 2018. His daughter, Cayleigh, is named after his childhood influences, Bruce Lee and Stan Lee. Joe's other influences stretch from Poe, Doyle, and Lovecraft to King, Connolly, and Gaiman (and so many more). Not to mention other great stories found in comics, movies, television, and games. You can read more about Joe and Crystal Lake Publishing at www.crystallakepub.com or find him on Facebook.

Christina Bergling has been writing since childhood. More than anything, she is a horror author. Crystal Lake released her last novel, Followers. Limitless Publishing published her novel The Rest Will Come. HellBound Books published her two novellas, Savages and The Waning. She co-wrote Screechers with Kevin J. Kennedy. She is also featured in numerous anthologies, including Collected Christmas Horror Shorts, Demonic Wildlife, Colorado's Emerging Authors, and Graveyard Girls. Bergling lives with her family in Colorado and spends her non-writing time working in IT, hiking mountains, dancing, and sucking all the marrow out of life.

Patrick R. McDonough is an editor, writer, and the producer/co-host of the Dead Headspace podcast. His penchant for horror and history leads him down endless paths, growing his interest in forgotten stories. He's a New Englander currently living in South Jersey with his wife, sons, dog, chinchilla, and pig. You can find his short fiction in various anthologies through Death's Head Press, Silent Hill Press, Cemetery Gates Media, and Crystal Lake Publishing.
Twitter: @Prmcdonough

'Audacious stories marinated in macabre, magic and mayhem.'

From the heart of Scotland, **Natasha Sinclair** is an independent writer, editor and artist. Working under her brand 'Clan Witch' for her creative endeavours and 'Word Refinery' for editorial works.

Her writing is often woven with horror, sex and psychological elements. She loves to frolic in the darkness with folklore and the macabre and rich history of her homeland.

Art is unrestrained freedom, as is how storytellers choose to wield the fluid movement and global diversity of language to carve captivating and authentic tales that woe, excite or terrorise an audience. Sinclair passionately embraces that, painting original characters with true form, dialect and depth. The devil is in the details.

Sinclair is the co-conspirator of 'Brazen Folk Horror' with her writing partner, Ruthann Jagge. The Brazen Folk Horror duo's debut collaborative novel, Delevan House released February 1st 2023. Book II in the trilogy is underway. Keep up to date by subscribing to the #BeBrazen newsletter.

Mark Allan Gunnells loves to tell stories. He has since he was a kid, penning one-page tales that were Twilight Zone knockoffs. He likes to think he has gotten a little better since then. He loves reader feedback, and above all he loves telling stories. He lives in Greer, SC, with his husband Craig A. Metcalf.

John Boden was mostly raised in the mountains of Pennsylvania, in the small town of Orbisonia. He is a bakery manager by trade and finds a regular sleep schedule overrated. He currently resides with his beautiful wife and two sons, in a house sweetly haunted by the ghost of a beautician named, Darlene. He likes collecting lots of things and won't usually shut up about it. His writing is fairly well received and has been called unique of style. His work has been published in the form of stories in several anthologies and as novellas. He plays well with others as is evidenced by collaborative works with Mercedes M. Yardley, Bracken MacLeod, Kurt Newton, Brian Rosenberger, Chad Lutzke and Robert Ford. He's easy to track down either on Facebook or Twitter (JohnBoden1970)

R.E. Sargent is an editor, publisher, and the author of three novels, four novelettes, and many short stories in the genres of suspense, supernatural, and horror. He is an active member of the Horror Writers Association, the Alliance of Independent Authors, and the Community of Literary Magazines and Presses. His short story, "Lucy," was featured in the

2021 Splatterpunk Award–nominated anthology *If I Die Before I Wake Volume 3 – Tales of Deadly Women and Retribution*.

R.E. lives in the Pacific Northwest with his wife and their Chocolate Lab. And the rain. Lots and lots of rain. He is thankful that writing is an indoor activity. Find out more about R.E. at www.resargent.com.

Nick Roberts is a native West Virginian and a graduate of Marshall University where he earned his doctorate in Leadership Studies. As an active member of the Horror Writers Association, his short works have been published in various literary magazines and anthologies. His novel, *Anathema*, won Debut Novel of the Year at the 2020-2021 Horror Authors Guild Awards. His best-selling novel, *The Exorcist's House*, was released in 2022 by Crystal Lake Publishing. He currently resides in South Carolina with his wife and three children and is an advocate for people struggling with substance use disorders.

Kenzie Jennings is an English professor residing in the sweltering tourist pocket of central Florida. She is the author of the Splatterpunk Award nominated books *Reception, Always Listen to Her Hurt,* & *Red Station*.

Mark Towse is an Englishman living in Australia. He would sell his soul to the devil or anyone buying if it meant he could write full-time. Alas, he left it very late to begin this journey, penning his first story since primary school at the ripe old age of 45. Since then, he's been published in too many journals and anthologies to mention and had his work featured on many exceptional podcasts such as The Grey Rooms, No Sleep, Creepy, Tales to Terrify, etc. 'There's Something Wrong with Aunty Beth' is his latest release, a collection of twenty of his best short stories, wrapped up with a brand-new novella, 'Mother Dearest.'

Brennan LaFaro is a horror writer living in southeastern Massachusetts with his wife, two sons, and his hounds. An avid lifelong reader, Brennan also co-hosts the Dead Headspace podcast. Brennan is the author of Noose, the story collection Illusions of Isolation, and the Slattery Falls series. You can read his short fiction in various anthologies and find him on Twitter at @brennanlafaro or at www.brennanlafaro.com

Jay Bower is a horror author living outside St. Louis, MO in the forest of Southern Illinois. He spends his time reading, writing, and convincing his wife the dark stories he writes do not involve her.

One time punk-rock skateboarder and heavy metal kid of the 80s, Jay approaches his work with the same indie attitude as those early punk bands.

More info and links to all his books can be found at jaybowerauthor.com

Adam Millard is the author of twenty-nine novels, thirteen novellas, and more than two hundred short stories, which can be found in various collections, magazines, and anthologies. Probably best known for his post-apocalyptic and comedy-horror fiction, Adam also writes fantasy/horror for children and Bizarro fiction for several publishers. His work has been translated for the German, Russian, and Spanish markets. He lives in Newcastle-Under-Lyme, UK, with his wife, Dawn, and her cats, which were not his idea at all.

David Moody sold the film rights to his novel HATER to Mark Johnson (producer, Breaking Bad) and Guillermo Del Toro (director, The Shape of Water, Pan's Labyrinth). His seminal zombie novel AUTUMN was made into a movie starring Dexter Fletcher and David Carradine. Moody has an unhealthy fascination with the end of the world and likes to write books about ordinary folks going through absolute hell. Find out more about his work at www.davidmoody.net and www.infectedbooks.co.uk. Join Moody's mailing list to keep up with new releases: https://www.davidmoody.net/signup/

John R. Little is a Canadian writer with 23 books published to date. His best known books are *The Memory Tree*, *Little by Little*, *The Murder of Jesus Christ*, and *Miranda* (which won the Bram Stoker Award in 2009).

He writes horror, dark fantasy, and thrillers, among others, and whatever the genre, he enjoys piecing together dark stories.

Lycan Valley Publications is publishing *The Complete Short Fiction of John R. Little* in four volumes. If you like the article in this book, maybe consider checking out some of his work. John loves hearing from his readers, so feel free to drop him an email at john.little@telus.net

Alex Laybourne was born and raised in the east of England; a short 15-year sojourn abroad saw him come back home wiser and better prepared. A writer, a father, and a generally nice person, he writes words that are, more often than not, the complete opposite.

A writer of horror and thriller novels, he has published several titles over the years, honing his craft with each one.

An avid reader and a big fan of family time, he can often be spotted perched with pen in hand, scribbling a first draft, or jotting down ideas for future use.

Writing came to Alex at an early age, and he attributes the wordiness of Stephen King for his often obscenely long essays at school. After a few turbulent years, he has settled back home, with the love of his life, with a nice house in a quiet suburb where he can peacefully sit and write all the blood-chilling, spine-tingling stories his hideous mind can conjure.

As a father and a step-father, he believes in encouraging imagination and play, following dreams, and above all, believing in magic.

https://www.facebook.com/alex.leybourne

A 2X Splatterpunk-Nominated Author, **Steve Stred** lives in Edmonton, Alberta, Canada, with his wife, son and their staffy, Cocoa.

His work has been described as haunting, bleak and is frequently set in the woods near where he grew up. He's been fortunate to appear in numerous anthologies with some truly amazing authors.

He is an Active Member of the HWA.

Website: stevestredauthor.ca

Twitter: @stevestred

Instagram: @stevestred

Tik Tok: @stevestredauthor
Universal Book Link: author.to/stevestred

Simon Clark's novels, include Blood Crazy, Vampyrrhic, Darkness Demands, Stranger, Whitby Vampyrrhic, Secrets of the Dead, and the award-winning The Night of the Triffids, which was broadcast as a five-part drama series by BBC radio. Weird House Press have recently issued Simon's new collection, Sherlock Holmes: A Casebook of Nightmares and Monsters and a novel Sherlock Holmes: Lord of Damnation.

Simon lives in Yorkshire, England, where he can be seen roaming this legend-haunted landscape with a black and white Border Collie by the name of Mylo.

Gage Greenwood is the best-selling author of the Winter's Myths Saga, and Bunker Dogs. He's a proud member of the Horror Writers Association and Science Fiction and Fantasy Writers association.

He's been an actor, comedian, podcaster, and even the Vice President of an escape room company. Since childhood, he's been a big fan of comic books, horror movies, and depressing music that fills him with existential dread.

He lives in New England with his girlfriend and son, and he spends his time writing, hiking, and decorating for various holidays.

Mark Lukens has had several short stories published and four screenplays optioned by Hollywood producers. He is the author of many bestselling books including: the Ancient Enemy series, the Dark Days post-apocalyptic series, Sightings, Devil's Island, Followed, Four Dark Tales, and many others. All are available on Amazon. He grew up in Daytona Beach, Florida. But after many travels and adventures, he settled down near Tampa, Florida with his wife and son, and two stray cats they adopted.
https://www.marklukensbooks.com
https://www.amazon.com/stores/Mark-Lukens/author/B00G8GYUUG

Ash Ericmore lives in Kent in England. By the seaside. He rarely leaves the house. A hermit by any other name, he lives on a council estate.
Hiding from everyone.
Seen once in shadow on a wildlife documentary, many dubious articles have been offered in attempts to prove the existence of Ericmore, including anecdotal claims of observations as well as dubious video and audio recordings, photographs, and casts of his monstrous footprints.
He is founder of the Ericmorean Church of Splatterology.
He can rarely identify an arse from an elbow.

You can find him at www.ashericmore.com.

Jim Ody writes horror and dark mysteries that have endings you won't see coming, and favours stories packed with wit. He has written ten novels and well over a dozen short-stories spanning many genres.
Jim has a very strange sense of humour and is often considered a little odd. When not writing he will be found playing the drums, watching football and eating chocolate. He lives with his long-suffering wife, three beautiful children and two indignant cats in Swindon, Wiltshire UK.

Robert Essig is the author of eighteen books such as Baby Fights, Secret Basements, and Mojave Mud Caves. He has published over 160 short stories and edited three small press anthologies, one of which, Chew on This!, was nominated for a Splatterpunk Award. Robert lives with his family in East Tennessee. Links to my webstore: https://ressighorror.bigcartel.com/ Link to my newsletter: https://robertessig.substack.com/

Brian Moreland writes a blend of mystery, action-adventure, dark suspense, and horror. His books include Tomb of Gods, The Devil's Woods, Blood Sacrifices: Three Horror Novellas, Savage Island and They Stalk the Night. A lover of adventure and world

travel, Brian is currently living in various places and writing scary books and short stories.
http://www.brianmoreland.com/
https://www.amazon.com/stores/author/B002BM3020
https://twitter.com/BrianMoreland

Chad has written for Famous Monsters of Filmland, Rue Morgue, Cemetery Dance, and Scream magazine. His short fiction can be found in several dozen magazines and anthologies, and some of his books include: OF FOSTER HOMES & FLIES, STIRRING THE SHEETS, CANNIBAL CREATOR, SKULLFACE BOY, THE SAME DEEP WATER AS YOU, and THE NEON OWL series. Lutzke's work has been praised by authors Jack Ketchum, Richard Chizmar, Joe R. Lansdale, Stephen Graham Jones, Elizabeth Massie, and his own mother. He can be found lurking the internet at www.chadlutzke.com

Kevin J. Kennedy is a horror author, editor, and anthologist. He owns and runs KJK Publishing. He lives in the heart of Scotland with his wife and his three cats, Carlito, Ariel and Luna. He can be found on Facebook most days if you want to chat with him. If you enjoyed this book, check out some of the other books he has put together.

Other books by KJK Publishing

KJK PUBLISHING

PRESENTS
THE HORROR COLLECTION

LGBTQIA+ EDITION

Coming soon!